AND WE STAY

AND WE STAY

JENNY HUBBARD

DELACORTE PRESS

Visit us on the Web! randomhouse.com/teens
Educators and librarians, for a variety of teaching tools,
visit us at RHTeachersLibrarians.com

Library of Congress Cataloging-in-Publication Data
Hubbard, Jenny.
And we stay / Jenny Hubbard.—First edition.
pages   cm
Summary: Sent to an Amherst, Massachusetts, boarding school after her ex-boyfriend shoots himself, seventeen-year-old Emily expresses herself through poetry as she relives their relationship, copes with her guilt, and begins to heal.
ISBN 978-0-385-74057-9 (hc)—ISBN 978-0-375-89943-0 (ebook)—
ISBN 978-0-375-98955-1 (glb)   [1. Boarding schools—Fiction.
2. High schools—Fiction. 3. Schools—Fiction. 4. Suicide—Fiction.
5. Interpersonal relations—Fiction. 6. Poetry—Fiction.
7. Amherst (Mass.)—Fiction.]   I. Title.
PZ7.H8583And 2014   [Fic]—dc23   2013002236

The text of this book is set in 13-point Perpetua.
Book design by Vikki Sheatsley

Printed in the United States of America
10 9 8 7 6 5 4 3

First Edition

For the ones who stay

in Paducah and Jonesboro and Springfield
and Littleton and Red Lake
and Nickel Mines and Chardon
and Newtown and . . .

AND WE STAY

THERE ARE RUMORS THE DAY EMILY BEAM ARRIVES AT THE AMHERST School for Girls—in January, halfway through her junior year. She doesn't look like the other girls, who look like girls in magazines. She doesn't sound like them, either, and she wears different shoes. As she sits on a bed she's never slept in, in the first room she's ever shared, Emily announces to the tall, curly-haired blonde standing by the window that she's come from Boston. This isn't a lie. It is where she's stayed for the past month.

K.T. nods and looks down at Emily's feet. "What size shoe do you wear?"

"Seven," Emily says.

K.T. walks over to her closet and digs out a pair of navy-blue clogs with wooden heels.

"Here," says K.T. "Wear these."

Emily takes off her rubber-soled Mary Janes.

"They'll be a size too big," K.T. says, "which will make it tough to walk on those little pebbles out there, but at least no one will talk shit about you."

As Emily slips on the clogs, K.T. takes the black Mary Janes and drops them—*clunk, clunk*—into the steel trash can.

"You can wear your pj's to class if you want," K.T. says. "A lot of us do."

Emily takes in her roommate's casual elegance: the untucked white button-down, the purple cashmere cardigan, the necklace of tiny turquoise beads, the brown suede boots with scuffed toes. Emily looks down at her new giant feet. "I have to go to the bathroom," she says.

"Do you remember where it is?" K.T. points. "Just at the end of the hall."

In the bathroom, Emily sweeps her long hair up into a messy ponytail, which is the style here, she's noticed. In the morning—her first day of class—she'll wear the Harvard sweatshirt she got in Boston. As far as boarding schools go, Emily has no idea how Amherst School for Girls ("ASG," K.T. calls it—like *ask* but with a *g*) compares. Boarding school? It wasn't even in the realm of possibilities; it wasn't even on the radar screen. And by the time Aunt Cindy convinced Emily's parents that it was necessary, ASG was the only school that would take her, and that was only because there was an extra bed since K.T.'s prior roommate, Hannah, had been expelled for sneaking out late at night to meet townies.

"You're a Hart Girl now," K.T. tells Emily on their way to dinner.

"A heart girl?"

"Yeah," says K.T. "As in Hart Hall, where we live."

"Oh, right," says Emily. The dorm doesn't look like dorms she's seen in pictures or movies. It's a house, a sprawling Victorian one, painted gray with purple trim, tucked behind a high row of boxwoods.

"ASG was the wrong place for Hannah to begin with.

This place is about the mind, and Hannah, well, she was all about the body."

Townies. Dorms known as halls. Cafeterias called dining rooms. To survive here, Emily is going to have to learn a whole other language.

Maybe that's why the poem comes sweeping in that very first night at ASG. In the past, Emily Beam has written poems only when a teacher has required her to, but as soon as she lies down on her single bed under the slope of the old wooden roof, lines unspool like ribbons, and she can't fall asleep until she ties them into bows.

MAZE

At the start, she stands: an opening
between the high, chopped-off
hedges. She can walk, one
foot, then another,
over the little pebbles.

It all looks so English,
so civilized, until
the dead end.
The dead end. The dead
end. The wind lends
the hedge its own green
voice. But what human speaks
Hedge? What antiquated
map shows a girl
the way?

No exit sign in neon
points her out.
No bread crumbs
on a path. If only
she were a pencil
with an eraser, she
could draw herself
out.

Emily Beam, *January 15, 1995*

4

EMILY LOOKS OVER AT K.T., WHO, BEFORE SHE FELL ASLEEP, PUT ON earphones and listened to classical music that was so loud that Emily could hear it across the room. Emily should be sleeping, too. It is five o'clock in the morning, and in three hours, after a special assembly celebrating the life of Martin Luther King, Jr., she'll stand face to face with her first day of classes. If Emily had to tell somebody what happened in the Grenfell County High School library, where would she begin? How desperate did Paul have to be to do what he did? Emily will never understand it, never. Didn't he realize that when he pulled the trigger, the world would go on without him in it? Didn't he know that dead, he'd be nowhere?

Emily puts her head down on her desk, on top of the poem she has written, and closes her eyes. As she has done for thirty-four nights, she tries to read past the dark. Read into Paul. There was little crime in Grenfell County with its spread-out landscape. The most violent thing ever to happen in the history of Grenfell County had happened at the high school.

The high school to which she will never return. The day after she and her parents arrived in Boston, Aunt Cindy quietly suggested over chicken potpie that they find Emily a boarding school, maybe even one in Massachusetts, where she could finish out her junior year. Emily's parents agreed. It was not a good idea for Emily to have to go back home and deal with the whispers and stares and, of course, the memories.

Emily was stunned. It was straight out of the Brothers Grimm. Boarding school? Only orphans and screwups and spoiled rich girls went to boarding school. She would be despised there, made fun of. She would become the butt of every joke ever told. So Emily pitched a fit, which had no effect. She jumped around the dining room and kicked the couch in the den and slung all of the magazines on Aunt Cindy's coffee table across the room. She told her aunt and her parents that they were evil. When she told them she hated them, they stared back at her, stone-faced.

For a month Emily stayed with Aunt Cindy, who oversaw Emily's recovery by renting movies on a theme. The first trip to Blockbuster, they rented films set in Paris—Emily's choice. The next time, Aunt Cindy chose films about high school.

"You haven't lived until you've seen *The Breakfast Club*," Aunt Cindy said. The movie was about five high-school types who don't know each other very well and get stuck together in Saturday detention in their library.

Emily shook her head. "Is it really a good idea for me to watch something that takes place in a school library?"

"Emily," said Aunt Cindy, "you're seventeen years old. I think you're smart enough by now to separate fact from fiction."

That's the thing, though; Emily isn't so sure. A story gets told one too many times and facts melt away like pats of butter. Case in point: not even forty-eight hours after Paul died, people in Grenfell County were saying that he had tried to use Mr. Jim, the one-armed janitor, as target practice when the truth was that the two of them had simply passed each other in the hall as Paul made his way to the library.

Another case in point: a new girl shows up at the Amherst School for Girls after the holiday break, and rumor has it that this new girl got into major trouble at her old school. Why else would she materialize midway through her junior year at a place where she has no friends, no connections, no legacy? Emily and Aunt Cindy sat on the couch biding time until Christmas was past and the new year was under way, eating popcorn and watching stupid high school movies about nerds who prevail or virgins who succumb.

Before Boston, before ASG, Emily had wanted nothing more than to be loved by a boy. When she was fourteen, fifteen, sixteen, she had watched girls on the cheerleading squad sprout wings with each boyfriend. They became more beautiful, the beauty of confidence. For four months, Emily had it, too.

But here at ASG, she is surrounded by girls more self-assured than she, clean-looking girls who sleep next to photographs of their boyfriends and talk to them daily on the phone in the hall. Boys are kept at a safe distance. The girl who gave Emily and her parents the campus tour was quick to point out that there are dances nearly every weekend with boys' schools in the area, but Emily wants nothing to do with boys or dances. She wants nothing to do with poems, either, but in the long shadow of death, they creep in.

.   .   .

When K.T.'s alarm goes off at six-thirty, Emily is already up and dressed in her Harvard sweatshirt, a pair of Levi's jeans ("unfailingly safe," K.T. told her), and her one thick pair of socks. The clogs wait by the door as she sits at her desk, doodling.

K.T. rolls over. "Hey, look at you! Let me throw on some clothes. You've inspired me not to wear my pj's."

When Emily came down the stairs wearing white on the day of Paul's funeral, her mother told her to go back upstairs and put on black wool pants. Emily told her to go to hell. In the church, she sat hunched between her parents. Enduring the funeral was like wading through a dark-gray fog, the disembodied voice of Reverend Wright cutting its way through:

"Though his time with us was short, Paul Wagoner followed in the footsteps of Christ. . . . We will never know why Paul did what he did. . . . With God's help, and each other's, we will come to accept the not knowing. . . ."

Paul.

Paul.

Pall.

On December 12, as the sirens drew closer to the high school, the students were told over the intercom to stay in their classrooms or to get to one. Theories were generated: Mr. Dees, the band director, had a heart attack; Mrs. Ziegler, the ninth-grade geometry teacher, collapsed on top of the overhead projector after solving an especially difficult proof. No one mentioned Paul Wagoner. No one. Paul was on the football team. He didn't spend hours in front of the TV. He laughed out loud at his friends' jokes, even the corny ones. He drank milk at lunch. He didn't scowl or dress all in black. He was on the way to being handsome, a country boy who hadn't fully grown into his looks. He wasn't the most popular boy in the senior class, but he wasn't the least popular, either. He lived somewhere in the middle, like most teenagers. Practically everyone in Grenfell County went to the funeral. Paul's teachers and Mr. Burton, the principal, sat in the front pews off to the side. The Wagoners sat front and center: Paul's mother and father, some other adults Emily didn't know, probably aunts and uncles. Carey, Paul's little sister, squeezed in beside their grandmother Gigi. It was Gigi's gun that had done the job. Paul had stolen it on a Sunday morning when everyone else in his family was at church.

How weird Paul must have felt to sneak into his grandmother's bedroom and open her bedside table; how sad for him to take what was meant to be an anchor in a sea of loss after the death of Paul's grandfather. In the long parade out of church, Emily tried to smile at Gigi, but Gigi wasn't looking at anything—her eyes were closed. Standing at the back of the church was Mr. Jim, the school janitor. Emily had been thinking of him only hours before as she'd stood at her closet, wondering how he got dressed. Mr. Jim had only one arm—his right—and Emily decided she would try getting dressed without using her left one. The bra was impossible, so she flipped it back into the top drawer. The black wool pants had three buttons, but the white dress had a zipper, so on it went. The shoes Emily had wanted to wear, her Mary Janes, had straps, so the black rain boots would have to do.

Emily bent down, the fingers of her right hand stretching into the dark like tentacles. Those boots were in the back of the closet somewhere. She hummed snippets of made-up songs. (*These boots were made for walkin' to where a boyfriend lies in a coffin.*) Once she found the boots, she placed them on the floor at the end of her bed, the rubber holes gaping. She was going to stand on her bed and jump into them feetfirst, but what if she fell and broke her ankle? Her parents would have to drive her to the hospital, and then they'd all miss the funeral. Emily left the boots where they were and rolled herself back on the bed until it was time to go, when she would manage the boots with one hand.

Paul had told her that when he died, he wanted to be cremated. (*Ashes to ashes, dust to dust, all our lives gone to rust.*) She wanted to forget that Paul had ever told her anything. She wanted to crawl under the bed, fall through the floor, and forget all the facts.

Paul.

Pall.

In the dim light of the desk lamp, while K.T. is down the hall in the bathroom, Emily opens her dictionary and looks up the word: *pall.*

    1. a cloth, often velvet, for spreading over a coffin, bier, or tomb.
    2. a coffin.

3. anything that covers, shrouds, or overspreads, especially with darkness or gloom.

Pall, then, as in *pallbearers.* Eight members of the football team—Paul's friends, and Emily's, too. She doesn't want friends at ASG because then she'd have to lie to them. It's bad enough lying just to K.T., but what other way is there? Mazes grow ever higher when lies beget lies.

K.T. pokes her head in the room and motions. Emily slings her book bag over her shoulder and follows her roommate to the dining room, which is bright and noisy.

"I'm going to show you how to work this system," K.T. says. "Grab a tray. Now, I like my eggs poached, but only Hilly will make them that way, and you have to ask her nicely when the boss man isn't around."

"That's okay," says Emily. "I like my eggs scrambled."

"IdonotlikegreeneggsandhamIdonotlikethemSamIAm," K.T. says. "Oh, and by the way, they put dreams in the coffee." She reaches for a cup and saucer. "That's why it's so good."

"Cream?"

"Dreams." K.T. smiles. "Good stuff."

"They put dreams in the coffee."

"If I'm lying, I'm dying," says K.T., her brown eyes deep and smiling. "I started drinking it last November, and ever since then, I sleep like a baby, ironically enough. I snore, by the way."

"So I noticed," says Emily. "But it's not very loud."

Emily reaches for a cup and fills it. She's only had coffee once before, in Boston.

"Well, according to Hannah, I sound like a freight train, but she was kind of a liar and kind of a bitch. I liked her, though. Follow me."

K.T. leads Emily to a table in the corner.

"If you sit here," K.T. says, "no one will bother you. If you want to be bothered, sit in the middle. And if you want to get any studying done, don't go to the library. It's where everyone goes to gossip."

If Emily says it out loud, the word *library* makes her queasy, so she says *lieberry* instead, which sounds like a leafy spot in a sunny garden. On that last Monday morning with Paul, it was damp and cold. Emily was wearing a thick sweater with a pouch across the front, and as Paul led her away from the long tables to an alley of books, she put her hands in the pouch. She did not want to hold hands with Paul anymore. Two days before, on her seventeenth birthday, she had ended things between them.

Halfway into the stacks, Paul stopped, and Emily stopped with him. He seemed at a loss for footing, for everything. A patch of his hair rose up in one spot.

Paul shifted his eyes away to the books on the shelves. "You don't love me," he said. "The other day you said that you did, but you don't."

"Paul . . ."

He held up his hand to stop her, and to avoid her gaze, he pulled the book off the shelf and opened it. Emily was sure it was a complete coincidence, the book that he chose. Paul wasn't a reader. Literature confused him. Emily had helped him once write an essay on *Paradise Lost,* and Paul had been as lost as the Eden depicted in John Milton's poem.

"Hey, what do you know?" Paul said. "I opened right to a poem about a gun."

K.T. waves her hand in front of Emily's face. "Earth to Emily," she says. "Time for more coffee?"

"Sure," says Emily. "I could use some more."

BLUES

She can't sing America,
not anymore. Columbia,
the Gem of the Ocean, has
dashed itself on the rocks,
the shell of her cracked
and scattered, and if it weren't
for the sea shining wide with hope,
she'd have buried her eyes,
two blue ones, in the sand.

Emily Beam, *January 22, 1995*

FOR A WEEK, EMILY HAS WALKED THE HALLS OF ASG. AFTER DINNER
tonight, she will call home just as she promised to do when
she stood with her mother at the front gate a week ago, and
she will tell her parents that she is doing fine. And in a man-
ner of speaking, she is. *Fine* means no highs or lows. *Fine*
means no trouble, no conflicts. She has avoided K.T. and the
other girls by hiding out in the lieberry, which looks like
a church. During the break between morning classes, after
lunch, during the evening study period, that's where Emily
goes, mostly to the top floor, to a carrel by an arched window overlooking the quad. The lieberry isn't as loud and
abuzz as K.T. led her to believe. It's peaceful, in fact, and
that very afternoon, standing by the checkout desk, Emily
has what she could only describe to herself as her very first
religious moment.

Sun streams in through the high Gothic windows, illu-
minating the dust. For minutes she watches the motes rise
and fall long enough for the rising and falling to become one
with her breathing, long enough to see the full extent of the
damage. Her damage.

As if being nudged by a hand at the small of her back, she
walks to the card catalog and flips to *Dickinson, Emily*. There

are at least twenty books on the subject. When Aunt Cindy first mentioned ASG, she said it was famous because of Emily Dickinson, who had been a student there over a hundred years ago, back when it was called Amherst Academy. It was resurrected as Amherst School for Girls in 1961, a hundred years after it closed, by a couple of poetry-loving sisters who never married.

Emily Beam knows something about Emily Dickinson from her English class at Grenfell County High. Emily Dickinson wrote 1,775 poems, a fact easy to remember because it's one less than 1776, the year America was born. As Emily Beam makes her way to the shelves of Dickinson books, she hopes that the collected poems contain a subject index; otherwise, she has no idea how to find the one poem she is looking for. Ms. Albright, her teacher, said that Dickinson didn't title her poems; she, or someone else, numbered them.

The Complete Poems of Emily Dickinson, edited by Thomas H. Johnson, looks thick and promising. "Gun, loaded, 754," the index reads. Emily turns to the page.

Is it the anger and frustration inside of Emily Beam that causes her to feel the anger and frustration inside of the poem? She doesn't understand all of it—in fact, she doesn't understand much of it. "My Life had stood—a Loaded Gun" doesn't sound like a poem that a shy woman, a woman who holed herself up in her bedroom during the day, would write. It sounds outdoorsy and violent: the eye of the barrel, the hunted doe, the volcanic eruption.

For a white-hot second, standing in the lieberry, Emily longs for the controlled chaos of the halls between classes, the low shouts of boys, the higher laughter of girls, the drumming on the metal lockers. But here, at least for the moment, it is empty and quiet, which magnifies the noise in her head. There are no school bells at ASG, and when she checks the clock on the wall over the circulation desk, she sees that she is going to be late for Sunday dinner if she doesn't leave that instant.

I'll be back, she whispers to the book as she slides it into its place.

.   .   .

For a while, instead of writing poems in the middle of the night, Emily reads them. She starts with Poem 1, a Valentine poem that calls out for the nine muses. *Oh the Earth was made for lovers,* it begins. It's a long poem. Emily thumbs through the book. Most of the poems are short. Emily decides she'll keep going: 2, 3, 4, 5.

By night, she reads. By day, she follows the rules—go to class, do your homework, study hard, eat three square meals, make polite conversation, do unto others. Emily has learned the first and last names of every girl in Hart Hall, and of the six other girls who live on the third floor, the pair in Room 12, Annabelle Wycoff and Waverley Graham, are the friendliest. K.T. assures Emily that it's nosiness, not friendship. "Plus," K.T. says, "they're cream puffs," which, at ASG, is a girl who uses hairspray and/or perfume and always wears makeup to class. "Even when it's five degrees!" K.T. exclaims. "Which is *not* weather to stand around and be vain in."

New England cold is textbook cold: blue and bracing and

bone-chilling. K.T. is accustomed to it, but Emily is not, and on January 30, after she's been there for two weeks, K.T. shows Emily how to order clothes from a catalog using a credit card, something that Emily does not have.

"You can pay me back," K.T. tells her. "Your parents give you an allowance, don't they?"

Emily nods, envisioning her little pool of babysitting money in the bank back home. Her parents have said nothing about an allowance—she's never had one—but she still has the hundred-dollar bill her mother pressed into her hand two weeks ago.

"You can't wear your Harvard sweatshirt every day," K.T. says, pointing to a purple sweater on sale in the J. Crew catalog. "Oh, and maybe you can order your own pair of clogs while you're at it."

Emily can't tell if K.T. is joking or not because K.T. doesn't smile when she says it. Emily smiles just in case and chooses a pair of short winter boots from Lands' End, also on sale.

The next morning in the dining room, when K.T. explains to Emily that the girls from New York City who sit together at a large round table are called "Algonquins," Emily asks K.T. why she doesn't eat breakfast sometimes with her other friends.

"I don't have a lot of friends," K.T. says, "except for the girls in the string quartet. But they're seniors, and they don't come to breakfast."

"They eat in their rooms?"

"Yeah. They share a triple over in Baker, and it has a small kitchen." K.T. sighs. "I wish we had a kitchen in our room. I'd cook for you. I'd turn you into a vegetarian."

"No way," Emily says. "I'm a meat-and-potatoes girl."

K.T. shakes her head. "You only think you are. Cheese, nuts, and coffee: I could live the rest of my life on that diet."

Emily laughs, thinking that K.T. might be joking. They have another cup of coffee before heading off to classes. Emily holds it together through most of them, but by Trigonometry, she is ready to lay her head on the desk and fall into the pit of sleep. She dreads the athletic period that follows—she's enrolled in Fitness for Fun—and then it's off to the dining room, where she's been assigned for the next two weeks to sit at a table with two history teachers and seven girls she doesn't know. She nods and smiles and pushes vegetarian lasagna around on her plate. She passes on the chocolate cake but drinks two cups of coffee.

After Tuesday dinners, there are club meetings, but Emily doesn't belong to a club. At the security desk in the main building, she signs herself out to go for a walk before study period. She's wired from the caffeine and needs to wander through a landscape, any kind of landscape, so that she can take apart her brain and put it back together again. This old New England town, with its shops and restaurants and large houses, will do just fine. She follows the sidewalk along the high stone wall surrounding the campus. If anyone were to ask her who her favorite character in literature is, she would answer Humpty Dumpty.

For as long as she can remember, characters in books have seemed more real to her than actual people. In the backseat of her parents' car on the way to Paul's funeral, Emily tried to pretend what she used to pretend on long rides with her mom and dad: that the car was a covered wagon and she was Laura Ingalls, on her way to the prairie. Outside, the clouds had hung low like the hammock she cocooned herself in one beachy summer a lifetime ago. *Where will we vacation this summer?* she wondered as she braided her hair into one straggly rope. *Are we still a family?* Maybe she could talk her parents into driving her to the prairie and leaving her there.

During the funeral, Emily chewed on the tip of her braid. To stop her, Emily's mother grabbed her hand and held on tight. When Reverend Wright spoke about an eighteen-year-old named Paul Wagoner, it didn't sound like he was talking about someone who used to be her boyfriend. The conclusion that Reverend Wright, the students, their principal, and their parents clung to was that it was no one's fault. Paul was going to do what he was going to do, and no one could've stopped him because God had called Paul Nathan Wagoner back home.

But Emily knows that God had nothing to do with it: it was her human error that caused Paul to end his life. With a loaded gun. With a big, fat, black exclamation point. As Reverend Wright prepared, with ancient Biblical words, to return Paul to the earth, Emily sent a letter to God, up to the rafters, up through the ceiling, up into the low clouds filled with rain.

Paul's funeral was forty-six days ago. She has not spoken to God since. *Tragedy binds,* one newspaper reported. *The silver lining of tragedy is that it stitches communities together again.* But as she walks the streets of Amherst, Massachusetts,

Emily has her doubts. Grenfell County was as devastated by this as it would have been by an earthquake. If the girl who caused it all, despite what others maintained, never returned to Grenfell County, would she still teeter on the fault line?

Amherst, Massachusetts, is so far away, so serene, a town at peace with itself even though the air at dusk is so cold that it can cut a girl in half. Emily notices a low puff of cloud, feathery and white against the darkening, and as she walks, the cloud seems to follow her. The day after she and Paul had sex for the first time, Emily rose early from her bed and put on the same coat she is wearing now. Still in her pajamas, she walked out the side door of her house. The hills in the distance, hugged by a veil of mist, seemed closer than usual, and she set out to reach them.

Emily lost her virginity in the middle of October in an abandoned barn. Paul got a blanket out of the back of his truck and spread it out on the packed-down dirt. He lit a candle he pulled from his coat pocket and, looking around for where to stick it, found a brick with three holes.

"It's going to be cold," he said.

"That's okay," said Emily.

"I'm kind of nervous," he said.

"Me too."

"I'm probably not very good at it."

"Me either."

"Oh, no," said Paul, helping her off with her coat. "You're perfect. You'll be perfect."

Walking toward the misty hills beyond her house the next morning, Emily locked the night before into place. The sex itself had lasted maybe a minute, but afterward, they had wrapped themselves up in the blanket for an hour or more and talked and kept each other warm. She wondered what was so perfect about her. Nothing, really. Her breasts were average, she had too many freckles, and her eyes were dull blue. She was average, like Paul was. His little sister, Carey, was the good-looking one in the family, with her luminous skin and high cheekbones, though she and Paul had the same stormy gray eyes.

Is Carey feeling like a lone survivor? Carey, who didn't get to escape like Emily, who had to go back to Grenfell County High School, to the three-story building that has stood on its own hill since 1921, a survivor of stock-market crashes and dust bowl storms and other major events in America that took place nowhere near it. In Amherst, the streetlights flash on, but the ghosts in a girl's heart, they stay.

LITTLE SISTER

Her mother woke her three hours early
for her brother's funeral when all
she had wanted, the only world
she could make for herself,
was the world of sleep.

The little sister stood in the shower
watching the short life of water.
Her brother had taken showers,
had taken his own short life.

The little sister dried her hair with a towel,
let it fall in her face. Over her head
she pulled the wool dress, black,
her mother had laid out on the bed,
and she hung inside of it.

She could hear the rain pecking
at the window. Chicken rain.
Peck peck, peck peck peck.
She had almost laughed
at how absurd it all was,
how water made mud
of the ground. How hearts
made mud of the world.

Emily Beam, *February 1, 1995*

EMILY WAKES ON GROUNDHOG DAY TO A SPLIT SECOND OF BLISSFUL ignorance, but then reality squeezes her heart with its tight grip. If she didn't have a schedule to keep, she'd curl back into the fetal position and try to sleep off the truth.

But there is one thing to look forward to after she rouses herself out of bed. At ASG, Emily has made a wonderful dietary leap.

Coffee. Coffee morning, noon, and night. A hundred and fifty girls drinking coffee. This would never happen in Grenfell County. It feels very European, like a description in a textbook for French class, which is much harder here than it was at Grenfell County. At ASG, she was placed in French II, and even though she did well on her mid-year French III exam, which arrived on January 5 at Aunt Cindy's in a thick envelope along with the rest of her exams, Emily is grateful for the wisdom that the headmistress, Dr. Ingold, showed in having her repeat the course. The classes at ASG are much harder, which is probably why the girls drink coffee all the time.

But today in French, Groundhog Day, Emily struggles. The fact of Paul's death and the fact of what she did in Boston join forces and wallop her. She has to tune out when the teacher, Madame Colche, shows the class a short film about Père Lachaise, the famous cemetery in Paris. Emily turns to a blank page in her notebook and practices her signature. It's time to change it up, give it more flourish. She increases the size of the *E* and makes the *y* bleed in to the *B*.

What had Emily Beam done to Paul's heart to make him do such a thing to hers? For Paul to want their story to end the way it did is beyond her comprehension, and the poems in her head, like her fancy new signature, flutter like flags of surrender.

Emily had read part of their story in the newspaper. On December 12, Paul went to his first-period class—Statistics. Eighteen minutes into second period, Western Civilizations, he raised his hand to go to the bathroom, and his teacher, Coach Stockley, excused him. But Paul didn't go to the bathroom. He walked down the hall. On the way to find Emily (the reporter presumed), he passed Mr. Jim, the janitor.

> "Paul was one of the few boys who looked me in the eye and spoke to me by name every time I saw him," said James Glass, custodian of Grenfell County High School for 25 years. "He was a nice young man. Such a tragedy."

Paul kept walking, past other classrooms, to Ms. Albright's classroom, where Emily should have been, but on that particular Monday, Ms. Albright had taken her AP English students to the library, which was right around the corner. So Paul entered the library where Emily was sitting with the rest of her class. Emily jumped when she saw him—she

25

knew he wasn't supposed to be there—but she got up from her chair and followed him into the stacks. He patted his backpack and told her he had a gun in it.

"That's not funny, Paul," she said.

He said, "I'm not joking."

"Yes, you are," said Emily. "Go back to class. We can talk during lunch."

There would be no lunch that day.

The gun Paul had stolen had room for six bullets. Three bullets would be used that morning; three bullets would remain. Mr. Jim, the one-armed janitor, had been a soldier in the Vietnam War. Maybe Mr. Jim knew things about Paul that Emily didn't. Maybe veteran soldiers understood death better than regular people, but if Mr. Jim had a clue as to why Paul killed himself, he didn't report it to the newspaper.

When the short film on the cemetery is over, Emily raises her hand.

"*Oui, Mademoiselle Beam,*" says Madame Colche.

"May I be excused?" Emily asks.

"*En français, s'il vous plaît.*"

"*Je voudrais aller,*" Emily says. "*J'ai besoin.*" *I would like to go. I have need.*

Madame Colche nods, and Emily, who sits in the middle of the room, hurries out, taking her book bag with her. She doesn't even know where the bathroom is in this building; she has to walk up and down the hall before she sees it, a tiny door labeled "WC."

Paul could have gone to the bathroom like he told Coach Stockley he was going to. He could have washed his hands and come back to Western Civilizations class and stared at the giant map of Europe on the wall until class was over, tuning out Coach Stockley, the most ignorant teacher at school. (He'd been telling students for years that the Gilded Age was the Guilded Age.) Paul could have stared at that large map, wondering what he would do once he graduated from high school. It was okay that he wasn't going to college; Mr. Wagoner hadn't gone to college, either. The plan was that Paul would take over the family tree farm, but not right after high school. After he went to the bathroom, after he stared at the map, after he graduated from Grenfell County, he could have gone out West.

He could have gone to Texas and been a ranch hand.

Or Alaska. And worked on an oil rigger.

Or California. All those vineyards.

He could have worked on a fishing boat in Washington State.

And then he could have come home, managed the farm, gotten married, and made a family. His parents could have been grandparents. His little sister, Carey, could have been a maid of honor, then an aunt.

Inside the WC, Emily locks the door and presses her hand to her mouth. The metallic taste of Boston winds its way back. She never even thought to ask the doctor what would happen to the fetus once it was flushed out of her body. Creatures the size of tadpoles weren't buried, were they? They were probably burned, burned up into the sky and reshaped into puffy clouds, tiny baby breaths bouncing along in the breeze.

Emily closes the toilet lid and sits down. From her book bag, she retrieves her notebook with the poems. She's

27

written three whole ones, but there are fragments of others scrawled here and there: *Sorrow fades with time. Classmates innocent as birds. Red ink spilled in the name of freedom.* She tears out all of the pages with words on them and returns her notebook to her bag. She folds the pages neatly into the trash can and stares at the ceiling, trying to fill her head with light, but all that comes is the first stanza of Poem 813, which she has not been able to get out of her head since she read it last night.

> This quiet Dust was Gentlemen and Ladies
> And Lads and Girls—
> Was laughter and ability and Sighing
> And Frocks and Curls.

Sighing, yes. Emily Beam is sighing for all time, just like Emily Dickinson. She checks her watch. There are ten minutes of class left, and Emily doesn't want to get in trouble, but when she tries to open the door, it doesn't turn. She jiggles the handle and bangs on the door and yells for help, but she's locked in, trapped in a water closet. When Emily doesn't return to class, Madame Colche comes looking. The lock is jammed on the outside, too, and Madame Colche tells Emily in a loud voice that she's called someone on the maintenance crew. By the time Emily is rescued, Trigonometry is over—all classes are.

"Come with me to the parlor, and we'll take tea before you go off to athletics," Madame Colche says. "I almost always take my afternoon tea alone, and it will be nice to have some company."

In the parlor, which looks just like a living room, Emily sits on an itchy brown chair. The talk is small at first. Madame Colche speaks in French, so Emily catches only some of it. As far as she is able to make out, Madame Colche grew up in Amherst, met a Frenchman in New York City, and married him. Because he would be gone so much, back and forth to Paris on business, he told Madame Colche that they could live anywhere she wanted.

"And I chose here," she says, gesturing around the room. She switches to English. "Being a hall mother keeps me from missing Henri. You girls keep me young. So, tell me about yourself, Mademoiselle Beam."

"*En français?*"

"*Anglais* is fine."

"Well," Emily says, "I've never been to France. But I'd like to go. And I'm an only child, so it was hard for my parents to send me here, so far away, but we live in a place where the school system isn't very good, which is why I'm no star pupil in French."

"Yet," says Madame Colche. "You're no star pupil yet. Give it time, Mademoiselle. I'm an excellent teacher."

"Oh, yes, ma'am."

"I hope you're starting to make friends here. I'm sure you miss your friends from home."

Emily pictures an empty chair at the round table of girls she sat with every day in the cafeteria, cheerleaders, mostly. Each girl was paired off with one other girl, a best friend. Emily's best friend, Terra, who was not a cheerleader, had moved away at the end of tenth grade, which suddenly made Emily the odd girl out.

"I guess they'll have to find someone else to be the middle block on the pyramid," Emily says. "I was a cheerleader."

"I'm sorry to say we don't have those here," Madame Colche says.

"Oh, that's fine. I've sort of grown out of it."

There is a knock on the door.

"Pardonnez-moi," says Madame Colche.

Emily hears another woman's voice and the door closing again. There is a long minute of silence before Madame Colche returns holding sheets of folded-up notebook paper.

"Mrs. Brooker found these in the bathroom when she was fixing the lock. She thought they might be yours. I took a look; it does appear to be your handwriting." Madame Colche holds them out for Emily to take. "So. You're a poet."

Emily shakes her head. "No," she says, "I'm just a girl who writes poems."

"And that doesn't make you a poet?"

"I think you have to be published to be a poet," says Emily, unzipping her bag and stuffing the folded-up pages into her notebook.

"I disagree," Madame Colche says. "Emily Dickinson wrote poems for years and years before she was ever published. But you would still call her a poet, would you not?"

"I would," Emily says.

"Pardonnez-moi," Madame Colche says once more, disappearing through what looks like a door to a bedroom. She flies back in, waving a sheet of paper in her hand. "Here," she says, handing it to Emily. "There's a poetry contest you should enter."

Sponsored by the Emily Dickinson Society, the flyer reads. *For girls aged 13–18.* At the bottom below the guidelines is an entry form.

"I'm a proud member of the EDS," says Madame Colche.

"Merci," says Emily. "I'll think about it. Oh, and *merci* for the tea, too."

Folding the sheet of paper into the back pocket of her jeans, Emily makes her mouth into a smile that she hopes isn't too fake and says, *"Au revoir."* Out on the quad, the clouds have lowered. When he came out of his burrow this morning, the groundhog did not see his shadow. It is raining now, a silvery rain that turns winter to spring. A heavyset girl Emily doesn't know passes by and tells her that the afternoon athletic period has been canceled, and the two girls share a joyful moment.

It was raining the night Emily and Paul first kissed, at a football party after the game. The rain had started during the fourth quarter, and Emily's hair and cheerleading sweater were still wet when Paul led her from the lights of the living room and onto the dark of the back porch. She hadn't planned to go to the party and didn't have a change of clothes, so she apologized for the dampness as Paul put his hands on her shoulders and pulled her close.

Emily used to think this was the beginning. Now she knows it was the beginning of the end.

As she climbs the three flights of stairs to her room in Hart Hall, Emily hears the hall phone ringing. By the time she gets to it, the ringing has stopped—somebody's boyfriend, but not hers. Hers is buried in the ground. Hers has a tombstone with Paul's name on it and two dates. A beginning and an end. In her room, at her desk, Emily opens her

31

notebook, the one with the poems in it, and writes another one, the second of the day. An hour later, when K.T. returns from her music lesson, Emily is fast asleep, folded over on her desk, used-up Kleenex scattered on the floor like roses tossed from a bride's bouquet.

ASHES

This is where her story
begins and ends. This is where
her story ends and begins.
In her story, the telling
is not linear. The telling
is a circle, the shape of earth.

If earth is a circle, there's no end;
she can't walk the plank of it
to sink in a bottomless sea.
So she throws away her insides,
which are burned
in the night, and the sky
sucks up
the ashes.

The same sky that once
held her dreams has stolen
her story. And the stars
will know just
how to tell it:
night after night,
over and over.

Emily Beam, *February 2, 1995*

AFTER DINNER, EMILY SIGNS OUT WITH THE OLD LADY ON DUTY AT the security desk and goes for a walk. The rain has stopped, but the sidewalks of Amherst are icy now that the temperature has dropped, so she shuffles along in K.T.'s clogs and her one pair of thick socks, which need to be washed. Emily is not a smoker, but just outside of the ASG gate, she finds an unopened pack of cigarettes on the ground. She walks a block before she tears back the thin layer of plastic and places a cigarette between her lips. She takes a pretend drag. The taste of tobacco blends smoothly with the aftertaste of coffee. She tucks the rest of the pack in the waistband of her jeans, pulls her sweater down low, and wraps her scarf around her head. Her nose is already numb, her fingers stiff. She shoves her bare hands into her pockets.

Walking through the icy dusk, the unlit cigarette hanging out of the corner of her mouth, Emily believes with a force that drives her forward that Paul never intended to use the gun. In this world of uncertainty, she has faith in one belief: that Paul never planned to shoot anyone, including himself. She clings to that belief. The gun was only a power play, a desperate, shortsighted, woefully misdirected attempt to prove his manhood. Here in Amherst, Emily has hardly seen a man; even the maintenance crew at ASG is composed of women. In the crystal-cold air so far away from Grenfell County, Emily can almost convince herself that her life before was the dream, and her real life began the day she moved into 15 Hart Hall.

She scoots down Spring Street, where the school is, and up Dickinson Street. Her fast walk must look suspicious, as if she's done something wrong. But she hasn't. Only her brain has, like wishing it had a pack of matches so it could set itself on fire.

On Main Street, Emily notices a sign in the yard of a large, yellow brick house—*The Emily Dickinson House,* it says, *Open Saturdays & Sundays 12–5.* She remembers the entry form in her back pocket and takes it out. Emily Dickinson, with her 1,775 poems, must have been running from something. Emily Beam opens the gate that separates the lawn from the sidewalk and carries the sheet of paper up to the railing of the front porch. Let another girl have it, she thinks. One who doesn't use her poems as places to hide. Let that girl enter the contest and be the center of the world for a day. Let her have fifteen minutes of fame because Emily Beam has had hers already.

When she tries to stuff the entry form inside of the iron scroll that attaches itself to one of the tall white columns, the overhead porch light winks. Emily jerks her head around. Is she trespassing? Does someone live here? She looks up and down, but all of the windows are blank and unfeeling. When she moves to leave, it winks again: on/off. And again. Emily flies back down the steps, almost tripping on her clogs, and slips and slides the three blocks back to school.

As she checks herself in at the security desk, Emily realizes she still has the paper in her frozen hand. She starts to throw it away there, in the trash can near the old lady's feet, but the lady is staring at her with a saint's possessed smile. Back in her room, Emily sticks the entry form into her notebook of poems and shoves the pack of cigarettes into the back of a drawer, behind her underwear and pajamas.

"I'm going to the lieberry," she tells K.T. "You don't have any matches, do you?"

"For what?" K.T. asks.

"There's something I need to burn."

"What?"

"Nothing important," Emily says. "Maybe I just feel like burning something."

"Oooh, pyromania," K.T. says. "Can I come?"

"Do you have any matches?"

"No. But if you find some, can I burn something, too?"

"Like what?"

"Like my grade report from last semester," K.T. says. "I spent too much time practicing the cello. Hey, wanna order pizza later tonight?"

"Sure," Emily says, thinking that she can break her hundred-dollar bill and pay K.T. back for the sweaters and boots.

"Is plain cheese all right?"

"Fine."

"Stephanie Simmons probably has some matches. She always smells like a chimney."

"I don't need them really," says Emily. "I can use scissors, I guess."

"You weren't going to burn your hair, were you?" K.T. asks. "You have great hair."

"I do?"

"Yeah. It's the color of horses. The pretty racing ones."

Emily walks over to the full-length mirror in between the closets and takes her hair out of its messy ponytail.

"You should wear it down more," K.T. tells her.

"Okay," Emily says. As she packs her book bag for a night of homework in the lieberry, she sees a book on her desk that wasn't there before, a biography of Emily Dickinson.

"Is this yours?" she asks K.T.

"Oh," says K.T. "Madame Colche stopped by after dinner. She said keep it as long as you like. She doesn't need it back anytime soon."

Emily opens the book to the slick pages in the middle. An image of Emily Dickinson, the one that Ms. Albright showed her class last fall, stares her straight in the eye. When Emily Beam shifts her head to the right, the eyes—bottomless pools—follow. When she shifts to the left, they follow. Emily Beam cannot escape. She reads the caption, which notes that the daguerreotype was taken when Emily Dickinson was sixteen or seventeen. The future poet looked sad and thirsty.

Thirst was the first sensation that returned to Emily Beam when Ms. Albright appeared behind Paul and demanded the gun. Paul did not give it to her. He lunged away, deeper into the stacks, leaving his backpack and the volume of poems he had pulled from the shelf in a lump on the floor.

Emily's mouth had been so dry that she couldn't speak.

"Help," she had managed to croak to her AP English teacher in a voice as tiny as a tree frog. "Help us."

PALL

Oh, yes, she could feel it
even though the bullet
had never stabbed her skin.
The bright white heat
burned at her core
where two lives
beat, and if he'd aimed
there and pulled the trigger,
red would have crested
like a broken dam
over her hands
as her last word rushed
up to her throat—*Paul*—
a sound that took no time
and also lifetimes.

                    Emily Beam, *February 3, 1995*

SINCE MADAME COLCHE GAVE HER THE SHEET WITH THE GUIDELINES for the poetry contest, the poems won't stop bursting in air. Like bombs, they blow up Emily's brain with images as she's walking along, just innocently walking over the little pebbles in her new black boots. Sometimes the words neatly arrange themselves into a Dickinson-like pattern.

> In the darkest Corner of the Place
> The Moment like a Riddle
> The Boy surrendered and then shot
> A Bullet through his Middle.

But if Emily can get the light to fall in just the right way, she can turn the bombs to blossoms. If she squints in just the right way, she can leave winter behind and arrive at a clearing, sunlit and green, where she stretches out on the grass, a bouquet of words gathered in her hand, and looks skyward.

Even at breakfast, poems rise into being, and sometimes Emily has to force herself to pay attention to K.T., just as she's doing now. It's the day before Valentine's Day, which, at ASG, is apparently almost as big a deal as Christmas. It doesn't seem to bother K.T. not to have a boyfriend, and it certainly doesn't bother Emily, who has sworn off boys. Plus, she has homework to worry about, way more homework than she ever had at Grenfell County High—three times as much.

"I'm glad Hannah isn't here," K.T. is saying. "She had, like, five boyfriends, and she'd enlist me to help her figure out which one to obsess over."

Emily has heard girls on the hall refer to Hannah as a ho-bag. "Five? Really?"

"Well, at least three. I liked her and everything, but she got around."

"Was she your best friend?" Emily asks.

"She kind of was, and she kind of wasn't. I mean, we did a lot of stuff together, but I don't know—it wasn't like we told each other our deepest, darkest secrets or anything."

Emily looks down at the remains of her scrambled eggs.

"I'm not sure I'm the 'best friend' type," K.T. says.

"Me either," says Emily.

"I might just like animals better than I like people. My mom and dad think I should be a veterinarian."

"Don't you have to go to vet school for that?"

"Yeah," K.T. says. "Which does not bode well for Yours Truly, who made a C in biology last year."

"College is a clean slate, though, isn't it? At least, that's what I'm hoping for."

"Why do you need a clean slate? You had to have had really good grades to get into ASG in the middle of the year like you did."

"Straight As," says Emily. "Except for a B-plus in tenth-grade biology."

K.T. raises a palm, and Emily high-fives it.

"I guess I could be one of those 'country veterinarians,'" says K.T. "You know, the crotchety type that thinks medical school is bullshit and teaches herself everything she needs to know. Did I tell you about that cat I used to have named Pablo? My mom and dad named him after Picasso, which was pretty ironic because at the time, we didn't know he spoke Spanish."

"Shut up," says Emily.

"No, I'm serious. Pablo liked to nap on my bed after dinner, and one time, when I was doing my homework—and before you make some smart-ass comment about that, yes, I actually do homework every once in a while—Pablo said '*pollo.*' Not 'meow,' like he usually said, but '*pollo.*'"

"Maybe he was hungry," Emily says. "Maybe you forgot to feed him dinner."

"I swear to God," says K.T., pushing her wild curls back from her forehead. "When I turned around, he was gazing at me like a sphinx. '*¿Cómo está, Pablo?*' I asked, but he didn't answer. Not that I expected him to, but, hey, stranger things have happened, wouldn't you say?"

"I would say." Emily nods. "Yes, I definitely would."

"Tell me one."

"Tell you one what?"

"A stranger thing that's happened."

"Well," she says slowly, "I saw a dog get hit by a truck once."

"That's not so weird," K.T. says.

"No," says Emily, "it was weird. Because it was like the dog *wanted* to get hit. It actually backed up onto the road. If it had kept moving forward, it would have been safe."

"Were you driving?"

"My boyfriend was. Ex-boyfriend."

"Did he cry?" K.T. asks.

Emily shakes her head and takes a long sip of coffee.

"I've never seen a teenaged boy cry," K.T. says. "Have you?"

"He didn't cry."

"Did the dog die?"

"Yeah," says Emily.

Emily had seen Paul cry, twice. On December 10, her birthday, the day she broke up with him, and two days later on the last day of his life. With her memory, she has tried to erase his tears, but no one could edit what she went through, not even her own amazing brain. What had happened on December 12, 1994, is stamped on there for all time exactly as it happened. Paul had tears on his face, tears in his voice, when he dropped the book he had pulled from the shelf onto the floor and grabbed Emily Beam's hands out of the pouch of her sweater.

"You can't do this to us," he said.

When she pulled her hands away, he bent down to the backpack, rummaging for the gun.

Emily watched in shock as he lifted it out. He held it for a moment in front of him, to show to her, then he pulled it in close, staring at it as if it were a creature he'd discovered on the beach. She held Paul's watery gaze.

"It's not loaded," she said. She was certain at first that it wasn't. If she'd really believed it was loaded, she would have grabbed it or dived for Paul's feet, something, anything, to keep him from doing what he did.

He stared past her, way past her, and that was when Emily got scared.

"Put it down, Paul. Or give it to me, okay? Give the gun to me." He didn't, and her knees shook so hard that she crumpled to the floor.

"It's our decision to make," said Paul. "No one else's. We love each other, don't we?"

Emily was crying now, too. "But I want to go to college," she said. "I can't do that if I have a baby." She shook her head. "Don't you see?"

But Paul was gone, sucked up into a black hole.

Emily said, "If you loved me, you would understand. If you really loved me, you wouldn't be so selfish."

Paul was now holding the gun out in front of him with both hands. Was he aiming it at her? It appeared that he was. She couldn't believe this was happening. Was it an out-of-body experience? A time warp? Was her brain completely done in because of all she had put it through over the past three days? She and Paul stared at one another like the trapped animals that they were.

His eyes clouded up, dark as she'd ever seen them. "You're the selfish one," he said.

It was the first time in Emily's life that she opened her mouth to speak and nothing, not even a breath, fell out. It was then, in the devastating silence, that Emily's English teacher, Ms. Albright, appeared. She stepped up behind Paul, quietly, like a cat.

K.T. takes a bite of poached egg (made by Hilly with love) and asks, with her mouth full, "What kind of dog was it?"

"I don't know," says Emily. "A mutt."

"And your boyfriend wasn't upset?"

"Oh, he was upset," Emily says. "He was shaking like crazy. The dog came out of nowhere."

Paul's attention had been drawn to the cows in the pasture on the other side of the road, dairy cows not bred for slaughter, soft and slow in the October sun. One of them was mooing. Paul had been explaining to Emily how he was learning to understand the way cows spoke to one another; he had worked that past summer on a farm that raised cattle. As Paul's truck swept around a curve, a black-and-white dog shot backward out of the tall grass and onto the road.

Paul jerked the truck to a stop, but he was too late.

"Oh, my God," he said. "Oh, my God." He looked at Emily. "The dog. Is it—?"

"I'm not sure."

Paul's hands were bouncing up and down off the steering wheel. "Will you get out and look? Please?"

Emily opened the door and took a few steps away from the truck. The dog lay on its side.

"It's not moving," she said.

Paul slid out from behind the wheel and walked around to where the dog lay, its legs stretched out in front of it. Its eyes were closed. It looked like it was sleeping. He bent down and touched it on the head. Blood trickled from the dog's mouth onto the asphalt as Paul shook the dog gently to try to revive it.

"I don't know what to do," he said. "It just came out of nowhere."

"I know," said Emily.

"It doesn't have a collar."

"It's probably a stray."

Paul looked up at her with big, blinking eyes. "You'll be my witness, right?"

Emily nodded.

"I don't think it was my fault," he said. "Was it?"

"No," said Emily. She watched as Paul lifted the dog into his arms and carried it over to the side of the road where the cows were. When he walked back to her, there was a smear of blood on his arm.

"I'll just leave it there," he said, "in case it belongs to anybody around here."

"It's a stray," said Emily. "There's nobody around except us and the cows."

Paul couldn't stop blinking. He looked back at the dog. He had laid it along the slope of the shoulder so that its head was higher than its body.

"Poor guy," said Paul. He covered his eyes with his hands.

Emily reached out and touched him on the elbow. "It's okay," she said.

"Nothing is okay," Paul said, his arms dropping to his sides. "Please don't lie to me, Emily. I know we haven't known each other long, but it'll all go downhill if we lie to each other."

Emily swallowed. She was about to tell Paul that it wasn't his fault, but maybe it was, and she didn't want to ruin the weight of the moment. A boy had never said such a serious thing to her before.

"It's sad when people have their dogs put to sleep," K.T. is saying. "The dog's owners are bawling and kissing all over the dog, and the dog smells their sadness and fear, which doesn't make sense to him because the regular kisses smell happy. How can the dog not feel even the slightest sense of betrayal? Better to be taken out by a car, just like that."

"Are you saying Paul did the dog a favor?"

"Read it however you like." K.T. shrugs. "So your boyfriend's name was Paul. I'm a fan of Pauls—Paul McCartney, Paul Simon, Paul Newman, Paul Revere." She sips her coffee. "RuPaul."

"Who's that?"

"That drag queen who's on talk shows all the time."

"I don't watch TV," Emily says.

"What? They don't have those in Boston?"

"Ha, ha," says Emily.

"Who doesn't watch TV?"

"I don't watch *much* TV."

"Why not?" K.T. asks.

"My parents are kind of strict," Emily says. "They say I have to study if I want to go to college because they can't afford to send me."

"How can they afford to send you here, then?"

Emily treads water. "My aunt's paying for it. See, she thinks that going here will give me a better chance of getting in to the college I want to go to."

"What college is that?"

"Harvard."

"But you're from Boston," says K.T. "Don't you want to spread your wings, expand your horizons, challenge yourself to move out of your comfort zone? Don't you want to embrace all those clichés the guidance counselors are always throwing out at us?"

Emily smiles. "Well, I'm not *from* Boston. It's just where I've been living for a while."

"Look, Emily. Annabelle and Waverley and the girls on the hall keep asking me what your story is. I'm only going to be able to put them off for so long before they begin their own investigation. And that could get ugly fast."

"I understand," Emily says.

"Want me to make something up?" K.T. asks.

"Sure, why not?"

"Are you serious?"

"Yeah," Emily says. "I don't care what they think."

"I'll make it good. I'll make it believable and all, but, oh, my God, this is going to be the most fun I've had all year."

K.T. offers up a high five, and Emily takes it.

"When I first met you," Emily says, "I thought your name was Katie. But then everyone kept saying it funny, like it was two words—Kay. Tee. So what do the initials stand for? I should have asked a long time ago, but . . ."

"But you didn't ask because you didn't want me to ask you anything back. Am I right?"

Emily nods.

"Keller True. Two age-old family names run together. I don't have any brothers, so—whoo-hoo! lucky me! the third daughter! the last hope!—I got them both."

"Well, Helen Keller Too Good to Be True, I wish I could tell you the sad, sad story of my checkered past, and maybe I will someday, but right now, I just can't."

"I knew you weren't from Boston," K.T. says. "Number one: you don't sound like you're from Boston. And number two: girls from Boston don't go around wearing Harvard sweatshirts."

"Why not?"

"Emily Beam Me Up Scotty, you don't advertise where you're from. You advertise where you've been. And even though it sounds like it, believe me, they're not the same thing."

. . .

During Trigonometry with the soft-spoken, square-haired Mrs. Frame, Emily imagines all the new identities she could invent. Not a single friend from home knows she got pregnant; not one of them knows she is here. And Dr. Ingold, the headmistress, is the only one at ASG who has been told about Paul and what happened in the Grenfell County High School library, but she has not been told anything about Boston because Emily's parents didn't tell her. They didn't tell anyone.

The day after Paul died, newspaper reporters called Emily's house. Mr. or Mrs. Beam answered at first, but after the third call, they turned the ringer off. When a policewoman showed up at the door late that afternoon, Emily sat in the living room between her mom and dad and answered the questions. Emily wasn't any help to the investigation. The gun and the use of it were total surprises—a boy caught in the heat of the moment. He had things to live for, Emily told the officer: he loved the trees under his care, and he was learning how to communicate with bovines.

As soon as the woman left, Emily flew into a rage. Her

mother and father had to grab her, hold her hands behind her back so that she didn't hurt herself. The police weren't interested in what Emily had to say about Paul and his trees. The officer had not asked a single question about what kind of boy he was—or what kind of girl she was to have fallen in love with him. The woman had wanted only the *when*s and *where*s.

Emily's parents tried to explain that the officer was only doing her job, but Emily was in no mood to be rational. As soon as the funeral was over, the Beams packed the car and left town with their only child crying in the backseat. Emily went through two boxes of Kleenex. Hours and hours later, when they arrived at Aunt Cindy's little house outside of Boston, her father opened the back door and helped Emily out.

"We're here, honey," he whispered. "Everything's going to be okay."

It was a lie, of course, but it was the first time in days that her father had been kind, and for a few minutes, the lie made Emily feel better.

When Mrs. Frame turns her back to graph a periodic function on the board, Emily reaches into her book bag for the biography of Emily Dickinson that Madame Colche lent her. Dickinson lived in a time of patriarchs. Men ruled the country, the church, and the home.

His Heart was pure and terrible, Dickinson wrote of her father, *and I think no other like it exists.* Edward Dickinson pulled her out of boarding school after one year, supposedly because she got sick so much, but Emily Beam wonders if it wasn't the father who had made his daughter ill in the first place.

Fathers are paradoxes—Emily Beam doesn't need a biography to tell her this. All males are. The summer before his senior year, Paul grew two inches. He came back to school with shoulders and wavy hair. He was six one when he started his senior year, and it was these changes more than anything that attracted Emily. She was changing, too. The melancholy that rose during the afternoon thunderstorms of her childhood was rising now in all kinds of weather, and after Terra moved to Ohio, it was much harder to find girls her age to relate to. They all seemed so sunny. Picking out Paul was like picking out the drummer in a band, not as cute as the lead singer or as flashy as the electric guitar player. She chose him to give some rhythm to her weekends, which had begun to feel longer than weeks, and aimless.

Lying down next to Paul, Emily measured herself by him. They aligned their torsos and their feet and their hands. Emily was five four then, and she is still five four, too short to be tall and too tall to be short. She is an in-between girl. Emily has always sat, if given a choice, in between other students, not in the front, not in a corner. Her teachers call on her because she's the one they see when they look out. And that's okay because Emily usually has an answer, even in subjects she doesn't care for, such as trigonometry. She is not short of opinions, and she has some ideas about a good many things, but she hasn't a clue as to how her days with Paul spiraled away from her so fast and so final.

It isn't Paul's touch that she misses the most. It's the smell of his truck: Old Spice and pine trees and brown leaves and apples. The smell of childhood and adulthood, rolled into one. There are places she needs to see again in the light of day, the graveled lanes and pull-offs where she and Paul had parked and made out. But for now, the walks at dusk through the streets of Amherst will have to do.

. . .

Emily wanders into the drugstore on Main Street to buy K.T. a small Valentine's Day gift. As Emily turns into the makeup aisle, she sees a girl with hair like wheat pick up a lipstick and tuck it in her purse. Emily makes a beeline toward her, and the girl whips around. It's like a scene out of a Western. Shoot-out at the O.K. Corral.

For the first time since Paul died, Emily feels powerful. She doesn't know who this pretty girl is, not yet, but she feels like she could kick her to Boston and back.

"I saw what you did," says Emily.

The girl plays dumb. "What do you mean?"

"You know what I mean. Put it back."

The girl reaches into her purse for the lipstick and returns it to the shelf. As she brushes the curtain of hair away from her face, Emily recognizes her.

"Are you going to rat me out?" the girl asks.

"I haven't decided."

"I put it back. The manager might not even believe you if you told on me."

"But then again, he might," says Emily.

"Assuming it's a 'he,'" says the girl. "You're in my French class, aren't you? You're that new girl."

"Oui," says Emily.

The girl makes a quick survey of the aisle. "If you say a word, I'll get kicked out."

Emily raises her eyebrows and swivels, but an untied bootlace trips her up, and the girl reaches out to keep her from falling.

"It was just a dumb lipstick," the girl says. Fear blazes in the girl's brown eyes, and the way the girl is still holding on to Emily's wrist—the way a small child would grip a mother—stops Emily from saying anything.

The girl follows Emily out of the drugstore. Why should this thief of a girl get off scot-free? She walks until she gets to the bench across the street from the Emily Dickinson House, and the girl sits down right beside her. It isn't until she reaches into her coat pocket for the pack of cigarettes and the matchbook she found on the bathroom floor in Hart Hall that she realizes that she forgot to get K.T. a Valentine's gift. After the wind blows out three matches, Emily finally gets one lit, touching it to the cigarette sticking straight out of her mouth. She inhales and coughs out.

"My name's Amber Atkins," the girl says.

"Emily Beam," says Emily in between coughs.

Amber points across the street. "Were you named after her?"

"Are you kidding? My parents probably never read a poem in their entire lives."

"My mom named me after a stripper she met in Las Vegas."

"So you're a thief *and* a liar," says Emily.

"We all are sometimes," Amber says. "Aren't you?"

Emily inhales, beginning to enjoy the taste of tobacco.

"My mom really did name me after a stripper."

"I'm not in a talking mood right now, okay? And I would offer you a cigarette, but that would be contributing to the delinquency of a minor. And you're already delinquent enough."

"I don't smoke," Amber says. "You're a minor, too, in case you haven't noticed."

"Yeah," says Emily, "but in my heart, I am very, very major, so . . ."

"You don't sound like most of the other girls at school. Where are you from?"

Emily takes the cigarette out of her mouth and makes a "zip it" sign with her lips.

"Oh, right," Amber says. "We're just gonna sit here and stare down the night."

Emily looks across the street at the stately yellow brick house, the kind of house she had always dreamed of living in. Large but not too large; elegant but not showy. Tall windows. Most of the houses in Grenfell County are small, boxy.

While riding in Paul's truck, winding through the woods and farms of Grenfell County, Emily began to take the female brain apart and piece it together again. Girls go back in their minds over things they wish they had said or done, or not said or not done, while boys put those things in a box with a tight-fitting lid. Girls think they can save boys in need, and Emily was no different.

The world is easier on boys, simpler. Paul had two choices once he found out Emily was pregnant: he could propose marriage, or he could pay for the abortion.

But the fact of the matter was that there was no choice, no second chance. Paul killed himself, so Emily has to go it alone.

"I guess we should head on back," Amber says. "It's almost seven-thirty."

Emily nods, lighting another cigarette and putting it in her mouth next to the other one. She inhales and coughs out, inhales again and sputters, wishing she could walk and smoke, smoke and walk, walk her mind to the sky, smoke her heart out of her body.

POEM OF THE MIDDLE HEART

You cannot hear me
through a stethoscope.
I do not say Ba-BUM, Ba-BUM.
If you cut the body open,
you would not find me.

I stick close to the invisible;
otherwise, I'd be hunted,
a sliver of food
on the dinner plate of the elderly,
silver as a fish,
a little doleful around the mouth.

No, my place is not
on the earth—it is
in the earth, an ancient vein.
It is everywhere
where you are,
It is everywhere—

at the intersection
of Young and Dumb,
and driven by the wheel
of need. No intellect
involved. No brain.
Just the rain of time
that keeps you skidding
back for more.

Emily Beam, *February 14, 1995*

EMILY BEAM WRITES HER BEST POEMS IN HER HEAD WHILE LYING ON her back staring through the dark at the ceiling while K.T. snores. Emily isn't sure what to make of K.T. While the two of them were in the bathroom a few hours earlier brushing their teeth, Annabelle Wycoff, who was washing her face, studied Emily in the mirror.

"Are you okay?" she asked. "You look sad."

Before Emily had a chance to pull the toothbrush out of her mouth, K.T. said, "Oh, didn't you know? Emily's an orphan."

"Oh, my gosh," Annabelle said. "Really?"

"Yeah," said K.T., making her brown eyes as wide as they could be. "Really."

Emily could tell that K.T. was being sarcastic, but in the mirror, Annabelle turned her eyes to Emily's. "But didn't I meet your mom? The day you moved in?"

"That wasn't her mom," K.T. said. "That was her guardian."

"But Emily introduced her as her mom."

"Wishful thinking," K.T. said. "Emily's much too devastated to tell the truth."

In the mirror, Emily narrowed her eyes.

"My gosh, I'm so sorry," Annabelle said. "How did your parents die?"

K.T. looked at Emily. "You want to tell her?"

Emily took the toothbrush out of her mouth. "In an avalanche," she said.

"They were skiing," said K.T. "In Switzerland."

"That is just awful." Annabelle turned to Emily. "Were you with them at the time?"

"No," said Emily. "I was here in the States, staying with my aunt in Boston."

"Her parents were on their second honeymoon," K.T. said. "They were very much in love."

Annabelle put her hand to her heart and looked at Emily with sad puppy eyes.

"Emily's hurt," K.T. explained to Annabelle. "She doesn't like to talk about it."

Without a word, Emily walked out of the bathroom and down the hall, past the huddle of girls by the phone waiting to talk to their boyfriends. When, a minute later, K.T. arrived, Emily refused to join her in her celebratory dance.

"I don't want to lie to anyone here," Emily said.

"It wasn't a real lie," said K.T. "It's not like she'll believe it."

"Why wouldn't she?"

"Because it's stupid."

"Whatever."

"Whatever yourself," said K.T., kicking off her suede boots. "Be that way."

Emily plopped on her bed, thinking of her mom and dad back in Grenfell County. She glanced at her watch. Her dad would be asleep downstairs in his chair with the radio on, and her mom would be upstairs in bed in her flannel pajamas, reading, which was where they were and what they were doing the night Emily returned from the party at Cole Hankins's house, the night it all veered off course.

First, there was what happened in Mr. and Mrs. Hankins's bedroom, and then, when a policeman showed up to shut the party down, Paul was the one to go to the door. Someone had seen the blue lights through the window and had warned everyone to hide their alcohol. When he let the policeman in, Paul did not lie when asked if the teenagers in the house were drinking.

"Tell you what," Paul said. "I'll take keys away from everyone who's in no condition to drive." The policeman stayed around to make sure it happened but didn't end up arresting anyone.

To Emily's surprise, Paul had been a leader that night. Maybe he was mature enough to be a father, but after that party, Emily felt about as mature as a tadpole. She had gotten drunk, the first time in her life she'd ever done more than nurse a beer for four hours. In Mr. and Mrs. Hankins's bedroom, the three beers she'd had downstairs were making the ceiling spin. After she and Paul did it once on top of the paisley bedspread, Paul wanted a blow job, and Emily said no.

"But it will turn me on," said Paul. "In a major way."

"That's what whores do," said Emily.

"Emily," said Paul, "you could never be a whore. You're a nerd."

"I am not!"

"You're, like, the one smart cheerleader. The hot *and* smart one."

"Is that why you like me? Because I'm a cheerleader?"

"No," said Paul. "No way. Give me some credit."

He rolled Emily down again on the bed. He was urgent and this time gave no thought to a condom. She didn't say anything; he was too far into her and too far gone. It was the only time they'd ever done it twice in a row, and afterward, Emily ran down the hall and threw up in the guest bathroom.

A lot can happen in a bathroom.

Before ASG, Emily never had to share one, but the bathroom in Hart Hall is hardly ever empty. She found the matchbook on the floor of one of the stalls. It was more than against the rules to smoke in Hart Hall—it could get a girl sent home. A wooden house built in the 1890s could go up in flames in a snap.

Emily gets out of bed and walks to the hook where her towel and flashlight are hanging. All AGS girls have hooks with towels and flashlights, their armor against a raging fire that would be started, no doubt, by one carelessly discarded match. Emily takes the flashlight to bed with her and opens the book Madame Colche gave her.

While the Civil War raged in the hills and valleys beyond her home, Emily Dickinson wrote. She was thirty-five when the war ended, a spinster still living at home, which wasn't unusual. Back then it was what unmarried women of privilege did.

Dickinson dashed off poem after poem, numbering them

to keep track. What she ended up with instead of a husband, instead of children, were words, thousands of them.

In the four months that Emily and Paul were together, they had sex fifteen times. Emily had been in Paul's bedroom twice, and both times, neither Mr. nor Mrs. Wagoner was at home. Her parents were strict, too, about allowing Paul in the house when they were away or already in bed, which was why Emily and Paul spent so many evenings sitting in the truck. Paul knew places to park on the back roads. They made out with the heater on; it was cold without clothes. But it had been thrilling, to be needed so wildly. The first time Emily rubbed her hand over his crotch, Paul came in his pants. He had been a virgin, too.

.   .   .

The next morning, as Emily is stepping out of the shower, Annabelle announces from the sink again how sorry she is for Emily's loss, her debate-team voice echoing off the tiles.

"I'm sorry for your brothers and sisters, too," Annabelle says. "If you have any."

"I don't," Emily says, wrapping her towel more tightly around her body.

"It's a good thing you're here, isn't it?"

Emily looks at Annabelle, who seems completely sincere.

"You have a hundred and forty-nine sisters at ASG. Isn't that great?"

Emily excuses herself.

"Don't hesitate to knock on my door if you need anything!" Annabelle calls as Emily walks fast, faster, down the hall to her room. When Emily throws open the door, K.T. is just waking up.

"Thanks to you, Annabelle now wants to be my guardian angel."

"You could use one," K.T. says.

"But she's a cream puff."

"Yeah, she is, but she aspires to be the first female president of the United States. It wouldn't be the worst thing, to have Annabelle watching over you."

"Why did you lie like that?"

"You lied, too," says K.T.

"You roped me into it," says Emily. "I couldn't just stand there like a mute."

"Come on, it was fun. *And* it will throw them off the trail."

"What trail? Who's *them?*"

"You would not believe the rumor mill at this place," K.T. says.

"Well, you sure gave it a generous feeding last night."

K.T. smiles. "Exactly. Annabelle is the Mouth. Once the story is out, all the other rumors will fizzle, at least for a while."

"I thought you said no one would believe it."

"They won't, not in their heart of hearts. But an orphan shipped off to boarding school because her hip, rich, very in-love parents died? Are you kidding me? It's romantic. The stuff of storybooks. And people believe what they want to believe."

"I need coffee," Emily says. "I need to think this through."

"It's foolproof," says K.T. "It will keep them occupied for a good long while. Trust me."

"I was taught never to trust anyone who says 'trust me.'"

"That's sad. Who taught you that?"

"My dad."

"Well, forget him," K.T. says. "He died in an avalanche, remember?"

Emily rolls her eyes. It is exhausting, nights of little sleep, days of being one against the world. While K.T. is in the bathroom, Emily sits at her desk and dashes off the poem that rained on her brain in the shower. Emily wishes she could write to Ms. Albright and tell her that the house where a great American poet lived, the one Ms. Albright loved most, is only three blocks away. Emily should go inside and buy a postcard and write in tiny, tiny print all she needs to say to the best teacher she's ever had. But where to begin? What do you say to the person who probably saved your life? Not only literally, but also figuratively. With Terra so far away, Ms. Albright's classroom was the one place at the start of eleventh grade where Emily could be Emily.

Unlike other teachers, Ms. Albright lined the windowsills with flowering plants. Her walls were covered with posters of books and movies that Emily had never heard of. Ms. Albright introduced her, introduced them all, to Ingmar Bergman and Bollywood, showing snippets of films every Friday but only if everyone in class had passed the reading quizzes that week. Every Monday at the start of class, Ms. Albright would read them a poem from the *New Yorker* or even a whole story. Sometimes she passed around the magazine so they could see the cartoons.

Ms. Albright told them memories of her own days in high school, which weren't that long ago, when everyone called her Tinkerbell because she was so small. Above all, Ms. Albright showed Emily that the life had a mind all its own, and that this life had its own separate beauty, its own separate magic. But what life is Emily living now? There are two girls trying to claim it, the Emily who used to be and another Emily, scarily unfamiliar. Sometimes, Spooky Emily can communicate only in meter and rhyme.

> A girl who lies alone
> In her single bed
> Cannot grasp the science of
> Her solitary head.

It is a sadder but wiser Emily who will rise each morning and eat breakfast with her roommate and go through the motions of being an orphan.

NEVER LAND

She rocks herself to sleep,
rocks herself awake, rocks
until she is one with a sky
deep as midnight.
The ground is not hers—
never was—and the only
light, the only light there is,
hums a high song
from the backside of stars.
Here in the dark, yes, here
is the cradle.

Emily Beam, *February 16, 1995*

MADAME COLCHE GIVES EMILY A SPECIAL SMILE WHEN SHE WALKS
into French, but Emily can barely smile back. It's Friday, almost the end of her fifth week of classes, and she feels like
a zombie. The coffee at breakfast hasn't stayed with her, and
she skipped lunch to go to the lieberry and write a poem
that had been tapping at the back of her brain all morning.
Emily almost asks Madame Colche for the leftovers in the
French press perched on the windowsill.

Amber sits in the back hiding behind her wheat-stalk
hair. As Emily slides into her desk in the middle of the room,
she catches Amber's eye. Amber looks away, but when Emily
turns toward her again a few minutes later, Amber winks at
Emily. Three times.

"Mademoiselle Atkins," Madame Colche says. *"Qu'est-ce
que tu as? As-tu quelque chose dans ton oeil?"* What's the matter with
you? Do you have something in your eye?

"Comment?"

Madame Colche repeats the question.

"Oui," says Amber.

"Qu'est-ce qu'il y a?" What is it?

"Regret. J'ai le regret dans mon oeil." I have regret in my eye.

The whole class turns to look at Amber.

"Hey, it's okay," Amber says. "*Ça va*, everybody. *Ça va*."

Madame Colche says nothing for a moment as Amber shakes her curtain of hair back into place.

"Amber," Madame Colche says in English. "Do you need to be excused?"

"No, ma'am."

Over the course of the class, each time Emily glances back, Amber is staring at her like she knows something she didn't know three nights ago. Emily feels the little bit of power that she wielded in the drugstore and on the bench slipping away. After classes are over for the day, Emily checks herself in to the infirmary so that she doesn't have to go to Fitness for Fun. She sleeps through dinner; she misses her walk. The nurse lets her sleep through the whole study period but wakes her so that she can get back to Hart Hall in time for check-in.

K.T. wants to talk, but Emily wants to sleep. She crawls under the covers and tries, but her brain won't stop showing its own little horror movies. In one of them, a large clock with swords for hands points to 9:18 as Paul lunges through the doors of the school library. Then, the floor opens like an earthquake. People and things, bookshelves and tables and notebooks, are swallowed up in the crack. In another one, Madame Colche chains Emily to the floor at the front of the French classroom and makes her dump out the contents of her backpack, which is loaded down with guns and boxes of bullets. Emily waits until she hears K.T. snoring, and she sneaks out of bed for her notebook and flashlight and crawls back under the covers.

Writing poems makes Time move backward, makes Time

move forward. Time will not stand still. Emily Dickinson raged her private rage by eschewing conventional punctuation or by capitalizing nouns that weren't normally capitalized; sometimes she did both. In the vaulted Space of Emily Beam's Mind, Ghosts hover like Clouds.

BUTTONS

Eight buttons on her blouse
like the eyes of daisies,
and his hands are giant
butterflies. Prehistoric
creatures of flight.

Underneath the buttons:
the girl. The butterflies
shift, soften in pursuit,
landing and staying
on hills made of skin.

The girl and
the butterfly boy—
they flutter over sheets
of white, arching and rolling,
the buttons abandoned
no longer strained,
no longer serving
the need.

Emily Beam, *February 17, 1995*

WITH THE AID OF HER FIRE-DRILL FLASHLIGHT, EMILY BEAM LEARNS that Emily Dickinson had been as interested in science as she was in poetry. She believed in step-by-step scientific proof, not grand leaps of faith. She believed in the smallest miracles of nature. Stalactites. A robin's trill. The dizzying speed of hummingbirds, each plodding step of the tortoise.

Emily Beam used to believe in those things, too. The survival of tadpoles. The transformation of caterpillars to butterflies. She knows that butterflies use antennae to lead them to potential mates. But what are humans supposed to use? What drew her to Paul, and he to her, was hard to say. They had walked the same halls for two years, and before that, they'd been at middle school together and in the same Sunday school class. What if they had just continued to coexist, as countless butterflies do?

Lying in Cole Hankins's parents' bed at the party, the party that ended it all, Emily asked Paul if he had ever loved another girl.

"It might not have been love," he said, "but it was something." That past summer, before Emily, there'd been a girl named Allison. Paul was working part-time at the farm where Allison's horse boarded. Allison, who was two years older, loved her horse; she did not love Paul.

"How could you tell?" Emily asked.

"I could just tell."

"But how?"

"She was always in a hurry around me," he said.

"Maybe you made her nervous," Emily said.

"No," said Paul. "It wasn't like that."

"So you never told Allison how you felt."

Paul shook his head.

"You pined away in anonymity."

"Yep," said Paul.

"Why?"

"I was afraid to risk it."

"Risk what?"

"It."

Emily kissed his naked shoulder. "You risked it with me."

"You don't feel like a risk."

"How do I feel, then?"

"Safe." He paused. "How do I feel?"

"The same," said Emily.

Which wasn't true, not entirely. Sometimes being with Paul felt safe, but sometimes it made her feel alone. He'd be drinking with his friends, and she wouldn't be, not whole-heartedly, anyway. If a trapdoor opened up in the floor, she could drop through it without Paul noticing until it was time to drive her home.

So Emily has decided that she won't go to any more parties. She is her own entertainment. Tonight, while a busload of girls from ASG are at St. Mark's Academy making out with boys in the bushes, Emily decides that she will stay in Room 15 with her books. She will order pizza and eat every slice.

The Soul selects her own Society— / Then—shuts the Door, wrote Emily Dickinson in Poem 303. A century and a half later, Emily Beam will follow in Emily Dickinson's footsteps.

"So you don't want me to sign you up for the Sadie Hawkins thing?" asks K.T. on their way to breakfast Saturday morning.

"Who's that?"

"It's the dance where the girls ask the boys. My God, Emily, you have lived a sheltered life."

Emily shrugs.

"But St. Mark's, being the elitists they are, call it the Snow Ball. It's the same thing, though. Come on. There'll be lots of guys there without dates. There's this one guy, Sam—"

Emily cuts her off. "I don't think so."

As they enter the dining room, Annabelle waves them over, but Emily pretends not to see.

"So what are you gonna do here all by yourself?"

"Study."

"Don't you need a break?"

"I can't afford a break," says Emily. "I want to get into Harvard."

"Harvard, Harvard."

"Though I doubt they'll accept me."

"Sure they will," says K.T. "Since you've made As on all of your tests—"

"Except for Trigonometry."

"Oh, and what was that? An eighty-six? You know, I've learned something about you girls who study all the time."

"What's that?"

"You all have a pathological need to anticipate the future."

Emily smiles a little. "So that's your theory, is it?"

"Yeah. School coincides with the worldview that if you pay close enough attention, you can beat time at its own messed-up game."

"You ought to write that down," says Emily. "Put it in one of those essays you're always turning in late."

"Hey, if the weather's nice, you want to go for a walk? Before I leave for St. Mark's?"

"Okay," Emily says. She starts to add the tag line that she and her Grenfell County friends used to say to one another: "As long as you promise me you won't do anything that I wouldn't do." Emily wishes she'd listened to her friends. She and Paul had been so historically dumb. They'd believed the bond would hold fast when all it took were a couple of crossed signals and parents to dissolve the glue. But some images stick, and the words that go along with them. So many things Paul told Emily, so many things Emily told Paul. It makes her want to weep a cupful of tears. Even if she writes 1,775 poems, she will not be able to preserve everything they did together, everything they said.

Emily spends the rest of the day, in between classes and sometimes during them, reading *The Collected Poems of Emily Dickinson*. She wants to write poems like these, simple but smart. Very, very smart. Every now and then, she'll come across one that sounds like a nursery rhyme that took a wrong turn down a dark alley. On her way to classes, Emily Beam walks to a beat in her new black boots and composes her own lost rhymes. But if she can hear them long enough to record them in her notebook—if they stay—even the faintest of poems can be found.

> I am just a girl on Earth
> Who writes her heart and brain.
> The world makes me a Poet; the world
> Gives me a name.
>
> When I die, they'll take my life,
> Transform it in a snap,
> Sensation wild and circus,
> As if I were a quack—
>
> They'll edit out my purest lines—
> Commas enter then.
> For clarity, is what they'll say.
> I do not write for them.
>
> I write for me and you and God
> In case He puts an ear
> Up to my heart and listens
> For stranger kinds of prayer.

.   .   .

On a cold but sunny Saturday, K.T. takes Emily on one of the trails that start from the campus at Amherst College, just a few blocks away. "The college has made all these into a wildlife sanctuary," K.T. tells her. As they walk through the brown fields, K.T. launches into a stand-up routine about all the weird people in her hometown, like the fat man who goes around showing anyone who passes by how far he has walked on his pedometer.

"He never, ever loses weight," K.T. tells Emily. "He's walked everywhere for almost twenty-five years. He gave up his car during the 1970s energy crisis."

Emily smiles.

"I wish you'd come with me tonight," K.T. says.

"Maybe next time," Emily says.

K.T. stops walking. "I want to be your friend. But sometimes I feel like you're using me. Using all of us."

"I don't understand," says Emily.

"Sure you do. ASG's your hiding place. And I'm your beard."

"My what?"

"Let me ask you a question. Are you a lesbian?"

Emily bursts out laughing. "Is that what everyone thinks?"

"Not everyone," says K.T. "It's okay if you are."

"I know it's okay," says Emily. "But I'm not."

"You'd rather have straight As than a boyfriend."

"Pretty much."

"I get it," says K.T. "I guess."

A bald eagle swoops out of nowhere over their heads and lands on a nearby fence post. "Oh," says Emily with a gasp. "Oh, wow. I've never seen one, have you?"

"No. Hey, guess what? We're no longer National Bird Virgins."

K.T. and Emily try to give each other quiet high fives,

but the eagle rises and disappears into the branches of a tree laced with new green.

"Did you know that Ben Franklin campaigned for the wild turkey to be our national bird?" K.T. asks.

"Actually, I did know that."

"It's a sign," K.T. says.

"Of what?"

"That you and I should room together again next year."

"Sure," says Emily.

"Maybe your work ethic will rub off on me," says K.T. "But that's not why I want to room with you."

"Oh, really?"

"You're gentle," says K.T. "But you have inner strength. It's comforting."

"I don't feel very strong on the inside." *As a matter of fact,* Emily wants to say, *my insides feel like a hurricane, and not the eye part, either.*

"There's a guy at St. Mark's I'd like you to meet," says K.T.

"K.T.—"

"Look, no pressure, okay? Whenever you're ready. He's like you, very Zen. He plays the cello. That's how I know him. He's had his heart broken, too."

Emily looks at her feet, watches them step across the stubbly grass at the same moment that something drops from a tree branch. She and K.T. bend down together. A pale-blue egg cracks open, yellow life slipping from it.

"Oh, no," says Emily and, without any warning whatsoever, the tears spring forth. K.T. puts her arm around Emily until she is able to stand and walk back to school.

ROBIN'S EGG

I am walking, I am out walking,
I am out-walking winter—when

a blue thing drops to the sidewalk,
whole, the size of an eye.

I look up—there's sky but
no tree to measure the tumble,

no mother to gather the fallen,
only color of day

spread out like a sea.
Neither human nor bird

calls out for its rescue,
vessel of being

useless now
as a tear.

Emily Beam, *February 18, 1995*

AFTER FINISHING A SMALL POEM AND A SMALL PIZZA, EMILY SIGNS HER-self out for a stroll. She heads toward Main Street, cigarettes and matches tucked deep inside her coat pocket. In the drugstore, she buys more batteries for her flashlight and a three-pack of thick socks so that she doesn't keep having to spend a whole dollar just to wash and dry the one pair she brought from home. And because the girl behind the counter looks to be underage, too, she takes her chances and asks for a pack of cigarettes, which the girl passes over without a word. Emily also buys a silly greeting card for K.T., nothing too sappy. The inside says, "Thank you for being you," and on the front is a photograph of a small boy and a smaller girl, their backs to the camera, gazing up at a very tall tree. It reminds her of a story Paul told her one November night when they were sitting in his truck.

"This one time when I was really young," he said, reaching over for Emily's hand, "Carey and I were building a fort together after school, and a golden maple leaf fell on my head like a little hat. I lifted it down and studied it. The leaf was so perfect that I shimmied up the trunk and tried to reattach it to a branch. I told Carey, who was, like, four, that the branch was the leaf's mother, and the leaf was her perfect child. Then Carey started to cry."

Paul paused.

"Why did she cry?" Emily asked.

"I thought it was because she felt sad for the leaf and the branch. But she said she felt sad for me. I asked her why, and she said, 'Because I know you, Paul, and you're going to feel really bad if you can't get the leaf to stay.' Which, needless to say, I couldn't. It floated back down to the ground. 'You should keep it,' Carey told me. 'Put it on your dresser.' But I said no—it would be lonely indoors."

"So what did you do with the leaf?" Emily asked Paul.

"I left it there on the ground just in case."

"Just in case what?" Emily asked.

"Just in case it was magic," said Paul. "I know it sounds stupid, but back then, I believed in that stuff. And the leaf was all golden and everything, so it wasn't out of the question."

Paul had been right: magic is not out of the question. Outside the drugstore, Emily heads toward the bench, lighting a cigarette and checking her watch in the glow. It's a little after nine, but because it's Saturday night, she doesn't have to be back till eleven. After smoking the cigarette down to the nub, Emily crushes the butt on the concrete with her boot and looks up at the sky, at the stars like tiny hands waving from a long way away. In the distance, a train rattles, but there's no sign of people. The Dickinson place is dark except for the porch light. Emily walks to the iron gate, which creaks but yields, and she steps slowly up to the house. The light doesn't wink at her this time. She leans back so she can see the second story. According to her book, the room on the left is where the poet slept and wrote, wrote and slept, for most of her life.

Emily Dickinson was gone from home for only a year, when she was sent to a girls' school ten miles away in South Hadley, a school now called Mount Holyoke College. When Emily Dickinson arrived there as a boarder at the age of sixteen, she was labeled as a girl "without hope," one of 80 girls out of 234 who had refused to stand up at assembly and profess their faith in God. By the end of the year, 51 of those had either changed their minds or caved under pressure. But not Emily. She and 28 other girls had stayed true.

This is the challenge: To stay. To stay true. That's what the poems are—a test to see how truthful Emily Beam can be. The blank page listens, but it can't talk back. Like the tree from which it comes, it has an innate ability to keep secrets. So far, Emily has kept her secret. Paul could have kept it, too. They could have lied to everyone and gone off and had the abortion—together. She and Paul could have rewritten history, sashaying their way into the future, putting the past in a box to store in the attic.

Which secrets did Emily Dickinson commit to paper, and which were too damning to share with the trees? Three weeks into her year at boarding school, Emily Dickinson had chosen to stay in her room while the rest of the girls went outside to see a traveling menagerie as it passed through the town. What was it that had prevented her from celebrating the bears and monkeys? The windows of the yellow house at 280 Main Street aren't giving anything away. In the dark, Emily Beam tiptoes across the front yard to the side of the

house, where she finds a garden. She knows she is trespassing, but she can't help it; something is drawing her with the
pull of a magnet. The moon drops out of a cloud, lighting
her way to a small cluster of flowers, their petals tipped with
silver. Early crocuses. It is so far from spring. Emily bends to
them, recalling a day long ago when she sat on her knees in
the snow outside her front door, puffing hot breath onto the
first crocus so it wouldn't die.

It is colder now than it was that day when her mother
had to trick her into coming inside. She had lured Emily
with hot chocolate. Emily takes her right hand out of her
coat pocket and, with a finger, traces the outline of each
purple flower. How can a thing so fragile push its way
through the frozen dirt? She looks up at the moon, but it
doesn't tell her.

Under its white, eerie glow, Emily feels something akin
to wind but stronger and softer rock her from side to side.
The motion is not at all scary because it's so familiar. She
does not have to fight to keep her balance; she allows it to
take her, take her back. Warmth drapes her shoulders like a
grandmother's shawl, and a hand as soft as velvet slides her
hair out of its ponytail and brushes it down her back. In her
ear, a voice whispers, *They are yours, all yours, go ahead.* But
the crocuses are too humbly triumphant. She leaves them
in the earth, her eyes hot with tears, a new poem burning
itself all the way down to her feet. She walks back to school
composing her verse, composing herself.

> "I'm Emily—who are you,
> Passing through the night?"

81

"I'm Emily, too. Lovely garden."
"Thank you kindly—it's my light.

People try to keep the dark
From entering the soul—
Though darkness is but who we were
Before the light blinked on."

In 15 Hart Hall, Emily transposes the poem, called "The Meeting," to a page with two other half-written poems and reads back over the one about the robin's egg. *Where's the hope there?* Emily thinks to herself. Although it's a Saturday night and she's alone, she is not entirely sure that it's loneliness she feels. With loneliness, you're trapped by the physical world, but with solitude, you're at one with it, as she was for that moment kneeling by the perfect crocuses. Emily is growing accustomed to the loneliness when it comes, announcing itself in the bottom of her soup bowl, in the water left running in the sink, in the twilit sky just before stars. In French class yesterday, she found herself hollowed out by a painting of a woman in a café, a portrait by Degas.

But it might be solitude rather than loneliness that surrounds her when she writes. Emily signs the card for K.T. and leaves it on K.T.'s pillow. Then she returns to her desk, turns to a blank page in her notebook, and makes a list of golden things.

Magic eggs.
Maple leaves.

Wedding bands.

Sunsets.

Silence.

For hours, poems roll in. Emily records them with the fountain pen that K.T. left on Emily's desk as a surprise. K.T. taped a note to the pen, tucking them both inside the book that Madame Colche had lent her. "This will make you feel more connected to E.D.," the note said. "P.S. Didn't she write with one of these?"

Emily wasn't sure what E.D. wrote with, so she tried to look it up in her book. It wasn't in there, so she walked over to the library and looked it up in another book. Emily Dickinson wrote with both pen (it didn't say what kind) and pencil and had a large pocket sewn into her favorite white dress for keeping stubs of lead and scraps of paper. The book showed a photograph of the dress displayed on a mannequin. As Emily Beam puts the gold tip of the pen (add that to the list!) to paper, she tastes apples, golden apples, though the words flowing out in black ink are bitter and musty.

SEED

The boy I loved
had the veins of the ancient.
He was eighteen, but also
a hundred and eighty,
Biblical and stubborn
as stone lodged
in the earth.

When the seed
spit its way to my womb,
I wanted to farm it,
watch over its growth,
and I was the mother,
my body the soil,
and so it was my
soil to keep.

My soil to keep.
And I would tend it
myself, root out
the weeds, rake
the dirt back
and forth, smooth
the soil over and
over and over and over
with my two bare hands.

Emily Beam, *February 18, 1995*

A GIRL HAS ONLY ONE LIFE, NOT TWO. BUT WHEN EMILY BEAM WAKES on Sunday at one o'clock in the afternoon, which is later than she has ever slept, she swears to K.T. that she has been reincarnated.

"Do you think I'm crazy?" Emily asks.

"You haven't even had your coffee yet, and you've lived two lives already?"

"Okay, look," Emily says, sitting back down on her bed. "I went for a walk last night, and something happened. Something really strange. Have you ever had déjà vu?"

"Yeah, a lot, but then we found out that they were actually epileptic seizures. You know those pills I have to take every morning? That's why I have to take them."

A voice on the other side of the door, Annabelle's, calls out: "Emily Beam? Phone call."

"Shit," Emily says, hopping up and grabbing her Harvard sweatshirt. "What if it's my mom and she told Annabelle who she was?"

"She's not really your mom, remember? She's your 'pretend mom.'"

"K.T., I swear you're on crack."

From down the hall, Emily sees the receiver dangling

by its twisted cord. "Annabelle?" she calls out. But Annabelle is gone. Pulling her sweatshirt over the T-shirt she slept in, Emily hurries to the phone and places the receiver to her ear.

"Hello?"

A girl's voice she doesn't recognize says her name.

"This is she," says Emily.

"It's Carey. Carey Wagoner."

Emily catches her breath.

"Your mom gave me your number."

"Carey. Oh, my God."

"I've been thinking about you. I hope it's okay that I called."

Emily hugs the receiver as close to her ear as she can. "Sure," she tells Carey.

"We didn't get a chance to talk after . . ."

Emily lets what doesn't need to be said hang itself on an invisible wire. In the silence, she hears the creak of a door. Annabelle steps out of her room and gives Emily a little wave.

"So how's your new school?" Carey asks.

"So far, so good. I've only been here for a month or so—"

"Same here. I went back to school after Christmas break."

"Me too," Emily says, watching Annabelle disappear into the bathroom.

"Everybody's being super nice to me," says Carey. "It's weird."

"I know what you mean."

"Even people who never spoke to me before."

"Well," Emily says, "people can be that way."

"Do you like your roommate?"

"Yeah, I really do. I got lucky for once."

"That's good. You deserve it," says Carey. "We don't blame you, Emily. That's why I called. Me and my mom and dad. We just started family therapy, and our homework is to tell somebody we know that we don't blame them for what happened to Paul."

"And you picked me," Emily says.

"Is that all right?"

"Yeah, sure."

Annabelle sweeps out of the bathroom, giving Emily a pat on the back as she passes. When the door to Room 12 opens, Emily hears a snatch of a song by Madonna.

"My mom and dad picked Gigi, in case you were wondering," Carey says.

"Oh," says Emily. "Okay."

"I was scared to call you," says Carey.

"You shouldn't have been."

"I'd like to talk. If you have a minute."

Emily looks around the empty hall. Annabelle's door is closed—all the doors are closed.

"Hey, look, Carey. Let me call you back when I have some privacy."

"Sure. I guess you've still got the number."

"Yeah," Emily says, "I've got it."

"I'll be home for the rest of the day. I'm playing softball now, but we don't practice on Sundays."

"Okay."

"Well, thanks," Carey says.

Emily sets the receiver quietly back onto its cradle without saying goodbye.

During basketball season, which started in early November, Emily had cheered for both the boys' and the girls' home games. Carey was the only freshman starter on the varsity team, and because she and Emily were kind of, in a roundabout way, connected, during the first couple of home games, Emily cheered longer and louder when Carey made a basket. Paul thought it was sweet. He told Emily she'd make a great mother someday. And then, lo and behold, she was pregnant.

On Thanksgiving morning, as Emily was putting on her bra, her breasts hurt. The bra seemed tighter, and the smell of pumpkin pie coming up from the kitchen, a smell Emily always looked forward to, made her nauseated. Before she could finish dressing, she threw up. During dinner at her grandparents' house, Emily stuffed herself with mashed potatoes and gravy, the only things that tasted right. Her mother looked at her sideways when Emily refused a slice of pie.

Emily's period was three weeks late, a fact she kept to herself for another two weeks until Thursday, December 8, when she was too tired to go to cheerleading practice and asked Paul to take her home. Instead of taking her home, Paul drove Emily to a drugstore in the next county over to buy a home pregnancy test. She made Paul go in while she waited in the truck. When he came back, he had two.

"We might as well make sure," he said. He handed her the bag. Clearblue Easy and BabyConfirm.

"They mash the words together," Emily said. "Why?"

"It sounds less serious that way."

"Less serious how?"

"It's like it's saying, 'Oh, goody! Having a baby's going to make life so fun!'"

Emily looked out the window.

"Listen, Em, if it's positive—"

"It won't be—"

"But if it is—"

"Paul, don't worry."

"Do you love me?" he asked.

Emily smiled. "Yes."

"Well, I love you, too," Paul said.

It was the first time he'd said it, the first time either one of them had. And it was true, wasn't it? They did love each other. The four months they'd been together had been uncharted frontier. Emily had never felt for another human being what she felt for Paul. The two of them had so much in common. They thought the same way about so many things.

They had the same favorite movie, *The Wizard of Oz*. Paul liked the scarecrow and knew his song by heart, and for the whole of second grade, Emily had made her mother braid her hair like Dorothy's. They were amazed to discover in each other a dislike for kids at school who played the victim, who blamed their screwups on other people or other things. Emily and Paul believed that there was a lot that was sad in the world, like how some boys had to join the army because they couldn't afford to go to college. Neither one of them could get over the fact that if either of their families had settled in a different town or a different country, they would never have met each other. It was frightening, the fact that life was that random.

"Say it again," said Paul.

"I love you."

"I love you, too."

"I need to go home," said Emily, staring out at the road in front of them, "so can we get this over with?"

Paul nodded and turned the key in the ignition switch. He said, "McDonald's is the closest bathroom, I guess."

"McDonald's it is," said Emily.

They went in together, and Paul waited at a table in the corner. When Emily came out of the women's room and told him, Paul blinked and swallowed.

"What do you want?" Paul asked.

"I don't know," said Emily. "Not a baby."

He smiled. "You're joking."

"I don't think so," said Emily.

"It's not right, what you're thinking."

"Who says?"

"A lot of people. God."

"But you don't believe in God anymore."

Paul looked stunned. "I never said that. When did I ever say that?"

"You haven't been to church in weeks."

"Because there's some stuff I need to work through. On

my own. Sunday mornings are, like, the only time when my family's not around."

"I don't want to talk about this here," said Emily.

"Okay, fine," said Paul. "We'll talk in the truck." He pointed at Emily's stomach. "Do you want anything to eat? You're eating for two now."

Emily fake-laughed. The news made her want to vomit. "God, no," she said. After Paul started to walk to the counter, she called him back. "Hey, Paul?"

"Yeah?"

"Don't tell anybody."

He stared at her.

"Promise," Emily said.

"I promise," he said. "Cross my heart and hope to die—"

"Stick a needle in your eye," said Emily, reaching out and touching his shoulder.

Emily had decided even before the tiny blue line revealed itself that she would include her parents on any decision she might need to make. Whatever the outcome, she was going to go about this in the most responsible and right way she could—she was going to be a grown-up even though she felt like a child. Growing up, her grandmother had told her, was one step forward, two steps back, and there was nothing her grandmother had ever said to Emily that wasn't true. Emily would tell her mother first, and let her mother tell her father, and she would brace herself for the wrath.

The sun was setting when they left McDonald's. Emily glanced at Paul, who was sucking on the straw from his milk shake. It almost made her sick, watching him. She knew then that they wouldn't be together forever, though she could tell what he'd look like at age forty. His brown hair would be mostly gone. He'd be fuller in the face, his cheekbones less prominent. His ears would be big like an old man's, and he'd probably wear glasses with little round wire rims.

Paul had brought her back a cup of ice water, which Emily tapped against the window in time to a song on the radio. Maybe she and Paul were in a commercial or a movie. They were driving toward a gold sun and pink sky, driving into a painting. That was it—they were models for an artist they just couldn't see.

"So was it your mom?" K.T. asks Emily when she gets back to the room.

Emily shakes her head. "A friend from home."

"You didn't talk very long."

"She had to go."

"You want some coffee? I was just about to make some."

"That'd be great," Emily says. "I've got a lot of work to do."

K.T. nods. "But you have to tell me about your reincarnation. We'll talk over coffee, okay?"

Emily waits until K.T. walks down the hall to get water before she grabs her pillow and screams, Edvard Munch–style, into it. She then grabs her book bag and because her boots take too long to lace, she slips her feet into K.T.'s clogs and rushes downstairs and out the front door. On the quad, girls are coming and going like nuns to and from vespers, and, as she makes her way to the lieberry, she becomes one of them, strange prayers whispering to her from the hedges.

The Bears put on their dancing shoes—
The Monkeys bow and grin—
The Tigers growl—the Lions prowl—
And I sit with my pen.

At the window of my mind—
I see it clear as day—
The girls aflutter in the streets—
Petticoats astray.

The charmers with their eely Snakes—
Tongues flickering like fire—
Make one girl scream—another faint—
And me burn with desire

For languages I do not speak—
And landscapes of the heart—
For boys with Secrets in their smiles—
Their lips like works of Art.

At her carrel by a window on the third floor, Emily records the poem that followed her to the lieberry, but she can't decide what to title it. "Circus"? "Desire"? "The Traveling Show"? Maybe she should just give it a number. Numbers, numbers. Like words, they have so many uses. Emily tries to forget Paul's phone number. She writes it over again and again, mixing the numbers up, replacing them with new ones. From her book bag she pulls out the poems of Emily Dickinson and opens to one of her favorites, Poem 185, which is short and sweet.

"Faith" is a fine invention
When Gentlemen can see—
But Microscopes are prudent
In an Emergency.

So Dickinson had it figured out in 1860, 135 years ago. Religion was made up by humans to justify why bad things happened to good people. If God had given Emily Beam a sign that He was on her side, she would have believed in Him. But God didn't go around tossing out clues like parade candy. Emily had had to turn instead to the likes of Clearblue Easy.

After Paul dropped her off at home that Thursday evening, Emily skipped dinner. She was queasy from the smell of McDonald's, and she wanted to get her thoughts together before she told her mother. She lay on her bed for over an hour, staring at the ceiling. When she came downstairs, Emily's mother was in the laundry room alone.

Emily walked straight in. "You're going to be mad at me," she said.

"How mad?" her mother asked.

"Very, very mad."

Her mother closed the lid of the washing machine and took a deep breath.

"You're pregnant."

Emily nodded.

"Tell me it wasn't under our watch."

"No, Mom. It happened at a party."

"Well, thank God for that, at least."

Emily rolled her eyes.

"How long have you and Paul been having sex?"

"It was the first time," Emily lied.

"Happy seventeenth birthday, my dear."

Emily looked down at her Mary Janes.

"After your father and I figure out how to deal with this," said Mrs. Beam, "you're grounded for life."

How right her mother had been: She *is* grounded for life. Grounded to her past, her doubt, her desk. It is hard to explore dark feelings in the light of day. How many poems did the other Emily write by candlelight after everyone else had gone to bed? In 1860, darkness had its place and its purpose. But with darkness, there is light; otherwise, how would you know where the darkness begins? Way back, before electricity was ever invented, people worked in the daytime and rested at night, but in the modern world, things are so upside-down. People work during the night and sleep through the afternoon. They work two or three jobs to keep their families fed, or work eighteen-hour shifts to keep the demons at bay, work and work and work because the sun hurts their hearts. And for them, the darkness is just like the light—indistinguishable.

Paul had not wanted to die. Emily will never understand it. She doesn't have enough imagination; she doesn't have enough ink. Darkness is patient. It lies in wait. It waited for Emily Dickinson, it waited for Paul Wagoner, and it will wait, too, for Emily Beam.

With her trigonometry book spread open in the study carrel, Emily gazes down onto the quad. One Emily wishes

K.T. would come find her; the other Emily wishes she wouldn't. The lack of caffeine is giving her a headache. On a typical day, she'd have had at least four cups by now. Emily stands and stretches and wanders downstairs to find the water fountain.

On another atypical day, a different library in a faraway state was the center of the national news. In the week that followed, the press roamed the halls of the school in search of commentary, in search of the definitive reason why Paul Wagoner did what he did. Stories about Paul were told and then printed. Stories of Emily Beam, too, found their way into the reports. A football mom had enjoyed watching her do back handsprings during games; someone else remembered that when Emily was seven, she had played the youngest von Trapp child in *The Sound of Music* back before the Grenfell County school system cut out its theater program.

And then there was the Emily Beam of December 12.

The papers reported that Emily's AP English teacher had felt a chill on the back of her neck when she glanced over at the table and saw an empty place where Emily had been sitting. So Ms. Albright went looking. She came upon Emily and Paul in an eerie pocket of silence. Emily was on her knees. "He's got a gun," she told Ms. Albright in a croaky voice.

"Paul," said Ms. Albright to the back of his head, "give me the gun. You don't want to do this. We know you don't." She held out her hand. "Here," she said. "I'll take it."

Paul shifted his eyes backward, but maybe not far back enough to see Ms. Albright's outstretched palm. He raised the gun straight over his head and fired the first shot into the ceiling.

Ms. Albright had been interviewed by several of the newspapers, Ms. Albright, who looked more like a student than a teacher with her curly red hair and her freckles. One reporter had asked Ms. Albright if she thought Paul had a plan.

> "If you're asking if Paul had any intention of hurting anyone," Albright said, "I would have to say no. It all happened so fast, but as far as I could tell, it didn't look to me that he was about to shoot Emily Beam. No, I don't think he had any intention of hurting anyone, not even himself."

Ms. Albright had proposed her theory to more than one reporter: that in the blinding chaos of the moment, Paul had panicked. He had run deeper into the stacks for an emergency exit, but there wasn't one. There weren't even any windows, just blocks of concrete stacked on top of one another to form walls. That was where, in the very back of the library, Paul had taken his second shot at one of those walls before he pushed the gun into his stomach and fired.

It was a library, not a lieberry.

A lieberry has windows with light coming through them. A lieberry is as cozy as a garden. The ideas it inspires are seeds that grow up to be flowers. This is why Emily isn't shocked at first, upon her return from the water fountain, to find a crocus laid across the open pages of her math book. Then a chill shimmies up and down her legs. She paces, back and forth, checking the other corners and carrels. No one. Not a soul but hers and the flower's, its purple head bright as birdsong.

GIRL AT A BEDROOM WINDOW

Tucked as one in a tree,
two wrens court for a full hour.
To the girl, this
is romance: the elegant
science of beaks, how they
distill softness, how they
parse into ribbons the language
of air—oh, it is quiet, the ruffle
of feathers, clicks to the tune
of sun. Years from now, she
will remember that sound—
two little swords—and she'll
wonder why she is here in this
used-up bed; she'll wish
for the window where she,
the leaves, their whole green
lives, nodded up and down like the sea,
the branch stretching herself out
for love.

Emily Beam, *February 19, 1995*

WHERE DID THE CROCUS COME FROM? FOR THE WHOLE AFTERNOON, Emily pinches herself: Is she real? She takes off K.T.'s clogs and her new drugstore socks and examines her toes, which look the same as they always have, but have they traveled somewhere and not told her? After Emily doesn't return to the room in time for Sunday dinner, K.T. comes looking. When K.T. finds her, Emily stands up from her carrel, first stretching her arms above her head and then stretching them out to K.T., who steps into them. The hug is long and stabilizing.

"I was worried," K.T. says.

"I'm sorry."

"Why did you leave like that?"

"I don't know," says Emily. "I'm really sorry."

"You said that already. Listen, I called Madame Colche. She's going to make you dinner."

"Oh, K.T., I wish you hadn't—"

"Well, I wish you'd come back when you're supposed to," K.T. says.

"I'm not hungry," Emily says.

"I'll go with you. Come on, you need to eat something, and it'll be nice."

And it is nice. While Madame Colche whips up mushroom and spinach omelets, Emily and K.T. sit on kitchen stools. "Let's play Favorites," Madame Colche suggests.

"How do you know about that?" K.T. asks.

"You give me little credit, Mademoiselle Montgomery," says Madame Colche. "I listen."

Favorites is a popular game at ASG; Emily has played it a couple of times with K.T. and with the girls at her dinner table. Madame Colche starts them off with food, Emily suggests movie stars (living and dead), and K.T. takes up books they loved as children. K.T.'s favorite is a toss-up, either *Harriet the Spy* or *From the Mixed-Up Files of Mrs. Basil E. Frankweiler,* and Madame Colche's favorite is *Hitty,* a book about a doll who lived for a hundred years. When Emily tells them about *The Secret Language,* she suddenly recalls how she used to beg her parents to send her off to the Coburn School, the girls' boarding school in the book. "How could I have forgotten that?" she says to them, remembering with shame the fit that she pitched in Aunt Cindy's living room. To herself, she thinks, *And K.T. is my Martha, and Madame Colche, our Mother Carrie, and I am Victoria North. Or did Victoria just come from the North? In any case, I am the new girl who learns a new language.*

During dinner on TV trays in the parlor, a fire in the fireplace, they talk about their favorite music. Madame Colche plays them a CD of live performances by Edith Piaf.

"She was thought of as a little sparrow. That's what *piaf* means—'little sparrow.'"

Emily pictures a large flock of birds swooping up from a field she and Paul rode by once in his truck.

"Piaf had such a sad life. She had to fight her way out with singing. You can hear that in her voice, can't you?"

"She sounds kind of manic," K.T. says.

"I think she sounds like champagne," says Emily.

"Spoken like a true poet," Madame Colche says. "Speaking of which, have you told K.T. about the contest you're entering?"

"No," K.T. says, sticking her tongue out at Emily. "She hasn't. Emily's not a big talker, in case you haven't noticed."

"I've noticed," says Madame Colche. "But we are here, Emily, any time you would like to talk."

Emily nods, her mouth full of buttered baguette.

"Emily is a gifted poet," Madame Colche says. "Extraordinarily gifted, in fact."

"I'd love to read some of your poems," K.T. says.

"K.T. plays the cello, and Emily writes. I have two of the very best artists at ASG right here, right now, dining with me in my parlor. If Amber Atkins were here, I'd have all three of you. You know her, Emily—she's in your French class. She's a wonderful painter."

"She's the sophomore with the hair," K.T. says, running her hands down the side of her face.

"*Oui.*"

"I saw some of her pieces in the school exhibit last year," K.T. tells Emily. "She's really good."

"I'll have to get you three together," Madame Colche says.

Emily slides her eyes toward K.T., whom she has not told about the lipstick incident. But why would she? Emily is beginning to understand something about girls: when big things have been swept with no warning right out from under their feet, they have to get a little back just to keep themselves tethered.

· · ·

For a week, Emily contemplates telling K.T. the whys of how she arrived at ASG. A couple of times, she picks up the hall phone to call Carey back, but as soon as she starts to dial, a girl walks by, and she hangs up. Late one night, she writes Terra a five-page letter, but then she remembers that she's left Terra's address back in Grenfell County. All she can remember is the name of the town and state—Winesburg, Ohio—so she seals the envelope and addresses it to herself. Emily hasn't talked to Terra since Christmas. Terra knows Paul, and knows what happened in the library, but what Terra doesn't know could fill way more than five pages. In the ninth grade, Terra and Emily put their hands on Terra's Bible at a sleepover and swore that they'd stay virgins until they were married.

On the last Sunday in February, a week after dinner at Madame Colche's, Emily closes up her poetry notebook and sets it on K.T.'s desk after K.T. has gone to sleep. Fourteen poems, fourteen little stories that make up one big story. There is another poem Emily must write, but it can't go in the notebook. It is too private. It needs to live under a mattress or a floorboard or in a locked drawer. As the whistle of the 2:00 a.m. train sounds low and long, Emily gets out a loose sheet of paper and closes her eyes, placing the tip of the fountain pen in the upper-left corner.

Was it too much beer or too much Paul that made Emily throw up in the guest bathroom at Cole Hankins's house?

She still isn't sure. After she scrubbed her mouth out with someone's dried-up toothbrush, she walked back down the hall to the master bedroom, where she and Paul had lain on Mr. and Mrs. Hankins's bed holding hands, listening to each other breathe. Paul rubbed Emily's stomach because she wasn't feeling well. He kissed her belly button and told her how sexy it was. He said he couldn't wait for summer so he could see her in a bikini.

When a girl loses something, she tries to accept the loss because it's what is expected of her. It is in her blood to lose. For example, a baby lives inside of a woman for nine months, and when it is born, it is no longer just hers. It belongs to the world. And there is the poor mother, trying to stitch up the emptiness. But the hole is too big, and the thread is too thin. That baby's going to get away no matter what.

MOTHER, ONCE REMOVED

There's a train to somewhere,
tiny baby.
Float away to a town
that loves the sound
of a train.

You can go
anywhere; you can't
go wrong if you
ride that sound;
the distant horn
will find you
your place.

And I, a stranger
by day and a stranger stranger by night,
I, who cut
you out
of the trap
of my body,
will listen,
always listen,
for the whistle.

Emily Beam, *February 27, 1995*

MONDAY MORNING, K.T. SEES THE NOTEBOOK. WHILE EMILY IS IN THE shower, K.T. sits at her desk and reads. Emily takes a longer shower than usual, and when she returns to the room wrapped in her towel, the notebook is sitting on top of Emily's pile of schoolbooks. K.T. doesn't say anything until they are both sitting in the corner of the noisy dining room with their breakfast coffee. Like a character in a play, K.T. reaches across the table for Emily's hand, squeezes it tightly in her own, and says, "Those are the best poems I've read in my whole life." She smiles the widest smile Emily has ever seen on K.T.'s face. "The robin's egg one is my favorite."

Emily waits for K.T. to ask questions, to offer up interpretations of soil and weeds and ashes sucked up into the sky, but K.T. doesn't. She doesn't even ask about the bullet. Emily pictures the purple crocus that was laid across her math book a week ago, the one she watched wilt and fade over the course of a long winter afternoon. Surely K.T. left it there, but where did she get it, if not from Emily Dickinson's garden? There are no crocuses yet on the grounds of ASG.

"Madame Colche is right," K.T. says. "You need to enter the contest."

"No. No way. What if I win?"

"Then we celebrate!"

"I threw the flyer with the details away," Emily lies.

"So get another one. Big deal."

"Let's just forget about the poems, okay?"

"No," K.T. says, "let's not."

"The poems are private. Madame Colche found out by accident. Neither one of you would have known anything about them if I hadn't gotten stuck in the WC. I mean it, K.T. Thank you for wanting to read them and all, but from now on, that notebook is closed to everyone but me."

"You're a bumped pumpkin."

"What's that mean?"

"It's ASG for 'odd duck.'"

"Odd duck."

"You've heard of that one, right?" K.T. asks.

"Yep. That's what people say where I'm from."

"And where is that, exactly?"

"Grenfell County, Nowhere."

"The girl who called you yesterday—is she from there, too?"

Emily nods.

"Let me guess. You don't want to talk about it."

Emily shakes her head.

K.T. stands. "More coffee?"

"Yes, please."

When K.T. walks away, Emily reaches into her book bag and lifts out her poetry notebook. She flips through the pages, unfolding the loose ones tucked into the back, the ones Mrs. Brooker recovered from the trash. What she sees in her words are contradictions and dichotomies and wild juxtapositions. What she witnesses is a girl on the run from her innocence.

Does she want it back? No, not all of it.

Does she want a giant eraser? Perhaps.

Does she wish for a maze-free mind? That might help.

As Madame Colche said the night before over coffee and dessert, fake it till you make it. Keep on keeping on. The only way to make sense of backward is to move forward.

· · ·

In French II that afternoon, Madame Colche hands each girl a map of the United States.

"You are going on a train trip," she tells them in French. "You will begin here in Amherst, and you can go anywhere that the train goes, as long as you travel to a place you've never been. Once you arrive, you will have an adventure. And you are going to tell the class about that adventure."

"*En français?*"

"*Oui, Catherine, en français.*"

"*Mon Dieu,*" says a funny girl named Lauren Dunlap.

"And," says Madame Colche, "you will take this trip with a friend, another girl from this class."

"I'd rather go with a boy," Lauren says.

Madame Colche ignores her. "I have assigned traveling companions according to birthdays. The girl in this class whose birthday is closest to yours will be your traveling mate, and, together, you will create an adventure for two."

Emily takes notes. Madame Colche has to repeat the instructions a few times until everyone in class understands the assignment in French. Unlike Emily's French teacher back home, Madame Colche uses her hands when explaining, which helps Emily understand better.

"We'll begin with January," Madame Colche says.

Emily sits and waits. She was born on December 10. As she watches everyone pair off, she knows no one wants to get stuck with her, the new girl with the halting French accent. By the time Madame Colche reaches October, there are only four girls left, and Emily sees it coming even before the announcement is made—she and Amber Atkins are going on a trip together.

But Emily does not want to travel with Amber. She knows in her gut that Madame Colche designed this whole game just to push the two of them into each other's paths. She thinks about asking if she can go to the bathroom and then not come back, but then she'll get Hashes (ASG for "demerits") and lose her sign-out privileges, which means no smoking after dinner, and Emily has been looking forward to a cigarette since breakfast.

So, slowly, she packs up the things on her desk and walks to the back corner of the room where Amber is waiting. Amber, who was born on December 11.

"Well," says Emily, "where do you want to go?"

Amber leans forward so that her hair veils her eyes and says, "Wherever they have the most drugstores."

"Ha, ha."

"Chicago, definitely," says Amber. "There's this famous art museum there, and I want to stand in front of two paintings: *A Sunday on La Grande Jatte,* a giant canvas composed of thousands and thousands of tiny dots of color, and *American Gothic.* Do you know it?"

"I'm not sure," says Emily.

"It's the one with the farmer holding a pitchfork, standing next to his sour-looking wife."

"Oh, yeah."

"I painted a version of *American Gothic,*" Amber says. "The woman and the man have switched places, and instead of a pitchfork, the woman holds a small white flag, like, for surrender. And I put this red hole, like, from a bullet, through her heart. And the man is younger. He's bare-chested and wears dog tags. And guess what I called it?"

"No idea," Emily says.

"*American Toxic.* Is that brilliant or what?"

"It's pretty brilliant."

"I gave it to my mom for her birthday—she was born on Halloween, which is way cool. It was in the school exhibit last year. The guy in the painting is my half brother Brandon. His dad and my mom got divorced before I was born. They got married in Las Vegas, and they took Brandon with them—he was three—and hired a stripper they met in a nightclub to babysit him. She's the one I'm named after." Amber paused. "True story."

Emily doesn't feel like arguing. "Okay," she says, "Chicago it is."

SMALL THINGS

I am the thief of small things.

The first small thing
I stole was a key chain
with a portrait of Jesus.
His eyes were closed,
and he was praying.

I am a small-time thief
stalking the drugstores of small-town America.
What do girls need
that they don't get at home?

The makeup aisles
with lipsticks the color
of candy: I want to eat every tube
in the privacy of my own room.
I want to stand at the mirror
and open my mouth
and bite down hard, peaches and pinks
glorified by the whiteness of teeth.

The key chain Jesus is still praying for me
year after year, drugstore after drugstore,
praying in the darkness
of my coat pocket.

Emily Beam, *February 27, 1995*

ALL AFTERNOON LONG, THROUGH TRIGONOMETRY AND FITNESS FOR Fun, where Emily walks fast around the oval dirt track on the playing fields, she thinks about Chicago. She has never been, but she knows that it's windy and next to a big lake. It was also home to many criminals, such as bootleggers who operated drugstores.

Emily has no desire whatsoever to go to Chicago. What was it K.T. said? It's not about where you're from; it's about where you've been. If K.T. is right, Emily should go to Las Vegas because she has gambled. That's what she should be advertising; that's what her sweatshirt should say. Yes, as far as high stakes go, Emily has certainly been there.

On the morning of December 10, Emily sat on her bed with her box of stationery and tried to put into words why she and Paul couldn't be together anymore. She still loved him, but it could not be. Emily's parents had sat her down after dinner the night before and had told her they would be leaving in a week for Boston. After school on Friday, the last day of the semester, the three of them would get in the car and drive to Aunt Cindy's. Emily and Mrs. Beam would stay with Aunt Cindy for the abortion, and Mr. Beam would fly home and then fly back to be with them at Christmas. Then the three of them—father, mother, and child—would drive back to Grenfell County sometime before the start of the new year.

"Before you go," her mother told her, "you'll want to explain things to Paul. It's only fair to him."

"Fair?" Emily screamed. "Fair?"

Her father shook his head in disappointment. Disappointment in her.

"Take a deep breath, Emily," said her mother. "Take a few."

Emily calmed down and said quietly, "I'm doing it in person. At least have the common human decency to allow me that."

Her mother turned to her father, and he jerked his head into a nod.

"Do it tomorrow, then," her mother said. "Best to get it over with so that we can all move on."

"Terrific," said Emily. "Gee, what a perfect way to celebrate my birthday."

Emily wrote the letter to Paul three times, three different versions, but she couldn't decide which one to give him. Before she went downstairs to ask to borrow the car, she folded up the letters and put them in a hat. Life—and this was what she was learning—was not something that could be controlled, no matter how smart you were or how smart your parents were.

The letter she picked out of the hat she copied over on a clean sheet of white paper. If Paul wasn't home when she got to his house, she would leave the letter for him. If Paul was home, they would go for a walk in the woods, and she would tell him face to face. She would break his heart, and her own, in the middle of all that nature, under the branches and the gray sky. Under God's watchful eye.

Emily drove over to Paul's house unannounced. She didn't call first. He wasn't expecting to see her until he picked her up at seven o'clock to take her to dinner, but she did not want to go out for her birthday. It would feel wrong, now that she was pregnant, to celebrate the fact that she was seventeen. It would make her feel like a hypocrite.

As she drove to Paul's, Emily scanned the sky. The birds and the leaves had flown from the trees. Everything was bare, and about to be bared. Snow had been forecast, and the clouds were heavy and low. Emily loved snow, but she hoped it wouldn't come until late that night when everyone was safely in bed.

Paul was home. Carey answered the front door and ran upstairs to get him, and Emily and Paul walked out the back door. They made small talk just as they had done on Friday at school, focusing on her birthday dinner rather than the pregnancy. The avoidance, the phoniness, when she and Paul had always been honest with each other, wedged in between them, even though they held hands. When she couldn't stand it any longer, she told Paul the news under the winter trees.

· · ·

On the last day of February, winter rages. Emily has a bad taste in her mouth after Tuesday's dinner at her new assigned table. Because of the sleet falling in daggers, she doesn't sign out for a walk. It's been a week and two days since Carey called, and Emily is terrified the hall phone will ring for her. She has to walk by it twice to brush her teeth. When she enters the bathroom, Annabelle Wycoff is standing at the mirror.

"Well, Miss Emily, you've made it through. February is the worst."

"Good thing it's not a leap year," Emily says.

"Baby steps," says Annabelle.

Screw those, Emily thinks. *Whatever happened to leaps?*

"Before you know it, exams will be here, and the seniors will graduate, and then we juniors will rule the school."

Emily does not want to think about hard tests or ruling the school. She is not a leader. She is a follower, always has been, and it suits her fine.

"Have you joined any clubs yet? We can always use an alternate on the debate team. Getting involved would definitely help."

"That's a great idea." Emily turns on the water full-force and scrubs her teeth so hard that she can't hear Annabelle talking, though Emily watches her mouth moving in the mirror. As Emily is rinsing, Annabelle's roommate, Waverley, rushes in but stops short when she sees Emily.

"Hi, Emily," Waverley says. "I hate that you didn't go to St. Mark's with us."

"Next time," Emily says.

"There are so many cute boys." Waverley mock-fans herself like a Southern belle.

Emily forces a smile. "Yeah, K.T.'s going to set me up."

Annabelle claps her hands together. "Oooo! Who with?"

"Some guy who plays the cello."

"Sam? Oh, Sam's adorable," Waverley says. "Very soulful."

Emily raises her eyebrows, and Annabelle and Waverley giggle.

"You're adorable, too," Annabelle says. "We're so glad Hannah got kicked out."

"Oh, yeah," says Waverley, checking her artfully messy ponytail in the mirror. "She was such a W-H-O-R-E."

So what does that make me? Emily wonders. Before she went to her first high-school party, Emily's mother warned her about being alone with boys. She told her that boys saw parties as golden opportunities to rack up bragging rights. When boys scored with girls, they were called players, but when girls scored with boys, they were called whores. It wasn't fair, her mother said, but neither was life.

"Hey," says Annabelle. "The girl who called for you last week. Was she a friend from home?"

"Yeah."

"She sounded nice."

"She is," Emily says.

"I bet she misses you a lot."

"She does, but she knows I'm at a good place."

"The best place," Waverley says. "And don't you forget it."

"I won't. Well, I've got homework to do."

High-pitched goodbyes echo off the tiles as Emily hurries down the hall. She glances at the phone, vowing to call Carey back on the more private phone in the lieberry after study period ends.

But at ten o'clock, another girl is already there in the telephone alcove. "Five minutes," she mouths to Emily, holding up spread-out fingers. Emily stands at the water fountain taking sip after sip, trying to be patient for five minutes.

What does Carey want to talk to her about? Does she know something new about Paul? If she does, is Emily sure she wants to hear it? Secrets can be more powerful than guns. Sometimes, after secrets are no longer secret, countless lives can be toppled—an entire city of fathers, mothers, sisters, brothers, aunts and uncles, grandparents, cats and dogs, you name it, blindsided by words.

Emily makes a deal with herself. She will walk outside. If she can see a hundred stars, she will call Carey. It is no longer raining, and stars pop out in every direction, hundreds of accusatory eyes. She counts in French, for practice, then she dashes up the lieberry steps, where she can see through the window that Five-Minute Girl is still talking. Emily runs back to Hart Hall, but Waverley is on the phone, practically making out with the receiver. In her room, Emily paces. When K.T. returns just before the 10:40 check-in, Waverley is still on the phone, and even if she weren't, it would be too late to call the Wagoners' house.

Emily lies on her bed and tries to slow down her heart, envying K.T., who falls asleep as soon as she pulls the covers up to her chin. For two hours, Emily stares through the dark at the ceiling. K.T. is snoring, but over her loud breathing, the sound of a boy's name takes its late-night toll.

Pall.

Pall.

Pall.

Emily tries to follow the sound down into sleep, but Carey's face keeps getting in the way. Paul drove Carey to school every day. So how does she get to school now? The bus doesn't run all the way out to the Wagoners' farm. And what music did Paul and Carey listen to on that final ride together?

Paul loved music. He was always introducing Emily to bands she'd never heard of. It is weird to think that Paul's favorite groups are making music that he will never hear. It is weird to think of Paul's mom and dad and Carey all riding to therapy. In what car? Not Paul's truck. What happened to Paul's truck? Emily pictures it parked on the side of the barn, rust on the passenger's door, frost on the windshield. It's been seventy-eight days, seventy-eight nights, almost twice as long as the flood Emily and Paul learned about so long ago in Sunday school, since Paul sat behind the wheel. Emily reaches out for her notebook and flashlight.

A NEW SOLAR SYSTEM

The sad mother
the sadder father
the saddest daughter
the saddest saddest brother
have holed
themselves off
from one
another

They are each
their own
planet
and outer
space

is
vast
vaster
infinite

Emily Beam, *February 28, 1995*

HOW HAD EMILY DICKINSON PUT IT?

> *Good Morning—Midnight—*
> *I'm coming Home—*
> *Day—got tired of Me*

Something like that. Seventy-eight midnights, and the feeling of shame over the choices she's made—over the one big choice—refuses to leave her. Her heart is anchored by it, her head stuffed full of what-ifs.

What if there had been another boy at school who wanted to tell her his secrets?

What if horse-loving Allison had loved Paul instead?

When Paul drove her to the abandoned barn, what if she'd said no, like she'd sworn on a Bible she would?

And there was, of course, the fact that she could have just left town without telling him she was going. Why did that never occur to her? He would have been angry—no doubt about it—but he would still be alive, and he never would have brought the gun to school.

What if Gigi had been sick in bed on that Sunday and had

had to stay home from church so that Paul couldn't have ever snuck into her room in the first place? Surely Gigi wouldn't mind being sick if it meant that her grandson would live. And if Paul were alive, Emily wouldn't feel so cut open, so cut up, so cut down.

So sew. Either way you spell it, on its own, the word looks wrong. Emily could write a poem about it, about how *sew* needs a subject, an object. About how a girl needs a duty to lock her in place. *So* if she sits at a desk, scrawls words on paper, are the words as lonely as she, or do they *sow* seeds into a soul across time, across centuries? Was Emily Dickinson ever able to thread the words together in such a way that she was beyond the need for stitches?

Emily reaches for the book on her bedside table and pulls the covers up over her head. She turns to Poem 812, the one she read to Paul before she knew for sure she was pregnant, and holds the flashlight over it.

On a Saturday in early December, five days before their trip to McDonald's, Emily and Paul sat in the truck in the Beams' driveway looking at the house, which Emily's father had decorated earlier that day with white lights that framed the front door and all of the windows.

"The whole Christmas thing," Paul said. "It's too much."

"Too much of what?" Emily asked.

"Too much of everything."

"I'm not sure I understand."

Paul sighed and pulled her closer. "People go overboard. They make things more complicated than they have to be. Even something beautiful like Christmas."

121

"Oh, Paul, that makes me sad."

"It makes me sad, too. I don't want to feel sad. There's all this light. I should feel happy, right?"

"Feelings are feelings," she said, repeating something her grandmother used to say. "There isn't a rightness or a wrongness to them. They just are."

"We raise trees on our farm. Saplings. How do they make it?"

"You help them," Emily said. "They wouldn't survive without you."

One of Paul's responsibilities was to measure the width of the Christmas trees, an act that resembled hugging.

"Then I go and cut them down," he said. "I mean, my parents talked to us a long time ago about what we do and why it's good and how the trees give back to the air and the cycle of it and all, but still."

"I want you to listen to something," said Emily, reaching into her backpack for her English book. "It was written around 1864, but to me, it seems like it could have been written right now." She read Paul the Emily Dickinson poem that she'd studied in class that week.

> *A Light exists in Spring*
> *Not present on the Year*
> *At any other period—*
> *When March is scarcely here*
>
> *A Color stands abroad*
> *On Solitary Fields*

That Science cannot overtake
But Human Nature feels.

It waits upon the Lawn,
It shows the furthest Tree
Upon the furthest Slope you know
It almost speaks to you.

Then as Horizons step
Or Noons report away
Without the Formula of sound
It passes and we stay—

A quality of loss
Affecting our Content
As Trade had suddenly encroached
Upon a Sacrament.

After she finished reading, Paul took the book from Emily's hand and kissed her palm.

"I like the way it sounds in your voice," he said, "but I don't get it."

"I'll teach you."

"I'm too dumb," he said, shaking his head.

"You understand trees." Emily kissed Paul's forehead. "You're not dumb. Poems grow just like trees. You'll see."

But he hadn't seen. He hadn't given himself time to see.

The night they sat in Emily's driveway, Emily tried to teach Paul something. What if she'd succeeded? What if there'd been some bit of knowledge set firmly down on pages that would have saved him?

"Dickinson's talking here"—she pointed out to Paul in the book—"about the transitory nature of light."

"I'm with you so far," he said.

She angled the book so that Paul could look. "Light visits less often than darkness. Most of the time, we're living in the dark."

"So true."

"The first word of the poem is like a seed," Emily said, thinking of the one that was likely growing inside of her. "And the last word of the poem is what that seed becomes. The rest of the poem is the poet changing that first word into something else. The word grows into something new, just like a seed grows into a tree."

"So light becomes a sacrament."

"Yes, exactly!"

"Okay, see? That's the problem. I'm not sure what a sacrament is. I told you I was stupid."

"I'm not sure I know, either," Emily said. "But I think it's something holy."

A sacrament, Emily knows now because she's looked it up, is a visible sign of God's grace. Emily Dickinson scoured her small corner of the universe in search of such signs. She lived in a time and place governed by Puritan values. To renounce Christianity publicly, as Dickinson did in front of her entire school, was to banish herself from society. She refused to call herself a Christian because she did not want to lie. Science, not faith, was her guiding light. Experimentation led to proof. Logic and reason were what she held dear.

But if that was so, then why were so many of Emily Dickinson's poems like little searchlights for God?

.   .   .

Walking to the dining room for breakfast, K.T. by her side, Emily considers what she is searching for other than a way out of her skin. As they scuttle over the pebbles, Emily hears lost rhymes rearranging themselves.

> In my life I watched God take
> Angels from my midst.
> I pinned some jasmine to my breast,
> Twined violets round my wrist
> While I raged inside myself
> Knowing what will be:
> When God takes way more than He gives
> He leaves the shell of me.

Maybe Emily Dickinson also heard poems under her shoes. Maybe she let this one stay so some other girl who came along could scoop it up, hold it in her palm.

"Rabbit, rabbit," says K.T.

Emily looks at her sideways.

"It's the first of March. Earth to Emily . . ."

"Is that another ASGism?"

"Seriously," K.T. says. "What rock have you been living under?"

"A really heavy one."

"You say it for good luck. It's supposed to be the first thing you say when you wake up on the first of the month."

Emily frowns. "Rabbit, rabbit?"

"Yeah."

"I think that might be a Vermont thing."

"No," says K.T., "it's an all-over thing. Why is the rock so heavy?"

"I need coffee," Emily says. "I can't talk without coffee."

"Can't or won't?"

"Sometimes I wish I were a little girl again."

"Are you homesick?" K.T. asks. "It's okay if you are. It happens here, especially in the winter."

"I'm not homesick," says Emily. "I'm nostalgic."

"I get that way at times," K.T. says. "Like when I want my mom here so she can tuck me in at night and wake me up in the morning. I hate alarms. Do you ever miss playing with dolls?"

Emily pictures her Cabbage Patch, Barbie, and Madame Alexander dolls in boxes under her bed at home. "No," she says.

"I think I'd rather play with them than with boys."

"You're funny."

"I'm totally serious," says K.T. "At the Snow Ball, as I was standing there talking to this guy, who was kind of an asshole, I started thinking about it."

"Why was he an asshole?"

"He never took his eyes off my boobs."

Emily smiles. "Get used to it, K.T."

"Oh, I'm used to it. I've had these things for ages. I'd give anything to be flat again."

"Yeah, right."

"No, really. I want to go back. Being a kid teaches you that you're the queen of your forest, and then whammo. You have to pack up your toys and start playing games with real people. I'm not so sure we're ready yet. I think we should play with our toys for just a little longer."

As they enter the dining room, Emily loses her appetite over the smell of sausage. "I'm just going to have coffee today," she tells K.T. "I'll meet you at our table." But the table is occupied, and Emily has to sit at one of the tables in the middle. While she's waiting for K.T., she opens up her poetry notebook just as Amber Atkins comes from behind and taps her on the shoulder.

"We need to finish our presentation," says Amber. "Is it okay if I sit here?"

"It's a free country," Emily says, adopting the official ASG attitude of a junior to a sophomore. At Grenfell County High School, the classes mingled more freely, but maybe that had more to do with boys and girls flirting than anything else.

Amber dumps her things—a dirty canvas bag and a large sketchbook—into a chair. "I'm going to get coffee," she says. "You need a refill?"

"I'm good," Emily says. In her notebook, she jots down a couple of lines and tucks it back inside her book bag. When K.T. arrives, and then Amber, the three girls make polite conversation about the dorm Amber lives in, Sweetser Hall, which was where K.T. lived last year with an exchange student from India.

"Jhodi never understood why Americans make such a big deal over the Indian/Native American thing," K.T. says. "The whole political-correctness issue wasn't in her repertoire. 'What's in a name?' and all that. She had the coolest accent ever."

"Political correctness is just another name for American excess."

Emily can't help but smile. Amber sounds like Paul.

"Before you know it," Amber says, "we'll be calling the homeless 'domestically challenged.' Look at Christmas, which now starts the day after Halloween. Look at the Big Gulp. Our country is so screwed up. Speaking of which, are we still going to Chicago?"

"It's a thing for French," Emily explains to K.T.

"You can come with us," Amber says. "We're taking the train to look at some art. Right, Emily?"

"Right."

"You know," says Amber. "We could go to Chicago. For real, I mean. The train station's just a few blocks from here."

"Right," Emily says again.

"I'm serious. What are you two gals doing for spring break?"

K.T. and Emily look at each other.

"Whatever," says Amber. "Hey, Emily, maybe we can work on this during lunch. I'll meet you in Madame Colche's classroom at twelve-thirty. *Ça va?*"

"*Ça va,*" Emily says.

Amber rises from the table, grabbing her stuff. "I'll catch you European Americans later."

When Amber is out of earshot, Emily says, "That girl is one bumped pumpkin."

"Pot, meet kettle, kettle, meet pot."

128

"You're really on a roll this morning, K.T."

"Not compared to Amber. I didn't know you two were friends."

"We're not," Emily says.

"It's okay for you to have friends other than me. Not that I have any friends other than you, but . . ."

"What about the girls in the quartet?"

"Oh, they're great. But they're all seniors, and they'll graduate before you know it, and then there I am again. Bereft. Like with Jhodi. I guess I shouldn't have put all of my 'friend eggs' in her basket."

Like me and Terra, Emily thinks.

"But Jhodi was really smart. And funny. And humble. She had seen so much more than the rest of us. After the novelty of having her around wore off for everyone else, she and I became close."

"I bet you miss her."

"I do. We talked about . . . stuff. And she was homesick the whole time she was here, but she stuck it out because she was only here for nine months. 'Only as long,' she would say, 'as it takes to make a human.'"

"I'm sorry you miss her," Emily says. "I'm sorry you got stuck with me."

"That's not what I meant."

"I know. But I'm still sorry about it."

"She and I agreed that feelings are the most important things," says K.T. "Much more important than facts."

"*Sorry* is a feeling, isn't it?"

"I've got to go practice. See you in the p.m.?"

"Okay," Emily says.

"Are you really?" K.T. asks.

"Am I really what?"

"Okay."

Emily nods. "I'm getting there," she says. She sips her coffee as K.T. takes her tray to the conveyor belt and heads back out into the cold of morning. In a few minutes, Emily follows the same path, wondering where the bread crumbs are that will lead her back to the girl she used to be.

TREASURES

The woods yield up their treasures
When you are but a girl.
Whole days under dappled trees,
A fairyland unfurls.

Mayapples with coquettish blooms,
Umbrellas to the moss;
Pinecones with their symmetry,
Feathers with their gloss—

They dare you to draw closer,
To see if you can see
Your magic self curled up within
God's rich poetry.

Emily Beam, *March 1, 1995*

EMILY AND AMBER ARE CALLED BY MADAME COLCHE TO DO THEIR presentation first, which, once again, arouses Emily's suspicion that her French teacher is up to something. During lunch, the two girls decided that Amber would do the talking about the journey to Chicago. While she does, Emily stands beside her, holding up pictures of the paintings they visit at the museum. Emily's job is to explain the journey back to Amherst. They take a side trip to the small town of Winesburg, Ohio, to visit Terra, whom Emily calls her *très bonne amie* even though Terra has no idea that Emily is now a boarding-school girl.

Or maybe she does know. If she's called the house, her mom or dad would have told her, but Emily is too ashamed to call Terra herself. Terra was as far from a ho-bag as you could get. She would never approve of what Emily has done.

That evening, Emily walks to the drugstore and, using up the last of her money, she buys three packs of cigarettes, which she will hide in the pockets of the bathrobe she never wears (her going-away gift from Aunt Cindy), and eight greeting cards celebrating friendship, which she doles out to K.T. over the next two weeks. Emily counts the days of March in animals—rabbit, rabbit; squirrel, squirrel; cow,

cow; dog, dog; dead dog, dead dog—and takes care to offer up, each morning with coffee, spoonfuls of emotion. The
feelings that she would otherwise give to her poems, she
gives to K.T. in conversation, the Hart Hall phone mocking
her with its silence every single time she passes it by. If she
were to walk by Paul's grave, that's how it would be, too.
Her footsteps find their metered pace up and down the now-
familiar path.

> The graves that stand on top of grass—
> Silence made of stone—
> Beckon to the girls who walk
> On melancholy bones.

.   .   .

On March 15, Emily buys a pack of crackers from the vend-
ing machine in the administration building and skips lunch.
The outside temperature is still below freezing. In the lieberry, she huddles into her notebook, intending to write,
but her hands are too cold to hold a pen for long. She ex-
changes it for one of the Dickinson biographies and sits on
her hands to warm them. It is much easier to make sense of
someone else's life.

A phone rings in the lieberrians's office, a sound that reminds Emily that she still hasn't called Carey back. It is beginning to feel as if there are signs everywhere meant just for
her. She reads that Emily Dickinson spent the most impres-
sionable years of her youth, from age nine to age twenty-
five, living not in the yellow brick house but in one on West
Street. *No wonder,* Emily Beam thinks. *How could a girl escape*

the darkness if she grew up on West *Street?* Every day dies in the west. Emily Beam is convinced that if Emily Dickinson had grown up on East Street, she would have been a much cheerier person.

Not to mention the fact that her room on West Street—now called North Pleasant Street (yet another sign!)—perched itself in full view of the town cemetery. Back then, in the years before modern medicine and antibiotics, there would have been funerals in the graveyard all the time. When Emily Dickinson was fifteen, her cousin Sophie, one of her closest friends, was dying, and Emily was granted permission by the doctor to enter Sophie's bedroom even though visitors were forbidden. She took off her shoes so as not to make noise, and when she gazed upon the face of her dying friend who could no longer speak, she was done in. She had to be dragged out of the room.

She did not and could not cry, she wrote in a letter to a friend. Sophie's thoughts and feelings had been so like her own that once her friend was in the coffin with the lid closed, a finality too deep to fathom, Emily retreated into herself. She was taken out of Amherst Academy and sent to live with her Aunt Lavinia. In Boston.

Emily Beam slams the biography shut. As swiftly as possible, but without calling attention to herself, Emily walks out of the lieberry and around the side of the building and down an alley that drops her out onto Webster Street. She heads to Main Street, turning left at the sign pointing toward the center of town. In front of the police station, an old man bends down to pick up an errant sheet of newspaper. As he rights himself, he smiles at Emily.

"Do you know where North Pleasant Street is?" Emily asks.

"If you'd taken ten more steps, it would have bitten you," the man says, pointing. "It's the next block down. Turn right."

She knows she is going to have to answer to Madame Colche and Dr. Ingold, and she'll probably earn herself a bucketful of Hashes or get herself campused—as in no walking privileges for a while—but she has to get there today, not tomorrow or the next day. She can't wait until this evening, because what if it rains? The clouds hang low, gray blankets over the blue sky, over the sun. She checks her watch—12:36—and walks fast. She knows from the biography that the house on Pleasant Street no longer stands, but she finds the cemetery, just a few blocks from Main Street, easily. A small sign points toward the Dickinson family plot in the center of the graveyard. Surrounded by an iron fence, the headstones mark the resting places of Emily; her sister, Lavinia; their parents; and their father's parents.

Right away, Emily can tell which headstone is Emily's. On top of it, people have left things: ribbons, roses, candles, feathers, a small china doll. Emily leans in to see what is carved into the marble. *Called Back,* it reads in block print, with Emily Dickinson's birth date above it: *Dec. 10, 1830.*

Even though Emily Beam is already aware that she and the poet share a birthday, it still sends electricity through her, to see the date etched in stone. In 1977, another baby given the name of Emily was born, Emily Elizabeth Beam, who has grown up to believe that when you die, you die. End of story. Emily Dickinson's story ended on May 15, 1886.

This quiet Dust was Gentlemen and Ladies
And Lads and Girls. . . .

Because Emily Dickinson died of an illness, she expected to die. Paul didn't. For him, death wasn't in the picture at all. When Paul brought the gun to school, he wasn't planning to use it, not on anyone. The morning had flipped over on top of him. Now he lived under a dogwood tree. The day he was buried, there were no buds in sight. But it is almost spring, and before the petals of a dogwood open fully, they look like little wings.

A sparrow, small and brown, swoops in and perches on top of the little china doll. For three breathless seconds, the bird pierces Emily Beam with its sharp, black eyes. Then it sings a high, clear song and flies away. Emily lowers herself on top of the ground and opens her notebook, her heart squeezed up like a fist.

THE SAFE WAY

Never relinquish your childhood,
your devotion to dolls,
to dressing them, pouring their tea,
bathing them, combing their hair,
tucking them into a nursery.

For they will teach you their way:
that there's safety in numbers,
in tasks with beginnings and ends;
they will make you believe
in the tightness of sleep.

You are not too old,
you are never too old
to unpack them from boxes,
lift them up, one by one,
catching each moment
when eyes blink open, blink wide,
lining them up on your unmade bed—
a chorus of wonder
at your return.

Emily Beam, *March 15, 1995*

EMILY WRITES UNTIL HER HAND IS NUMB FROM THE COLD. THE WIND has picked up, and her coat is in the lieberry. She checks her watch: two-thirty. Trigonometry class has started. She is going to fail a math test, but that is the least of her worries. She hurries back to campus, taking what she hopes is a shortcut through a park with a small lake. Sweetser Park, it's called, the same name as Amber Atkins's dorm. A lone swan floats, its neck folded into its white feathers. Around the lake, early daffodils curtsy and bow.

In the letter she gave to Paul, Emily had written that she loved him. She had sworn it. Yes, they had broken up for now, but she would come back to Grenfell County after her sentence in Boston was over, and they would see each other at school, and she would keep him in her heart until it was reasonable for them to be together again. But there was nothing reasonable about the heart, nothing at all. In truth, she wrote these things because she thought they were what Paul wanted to hear. How silly that letter would sound to her now. It makes her shudder.

In the cold air of winter, Emily and Paul walked out the back door of Paul's house under clouds brimming with snow. They entered the woods, scuffling over the fallen leaves, and

Emily broke the news. She told Paul that she was leaving for a few weeks. She told him that her parents were making her have an abortion.

"Oh," he said, nodding too fast. "Oh."

"What?"

"So you want an abortion."

"No." She paused. "Yes."

"Which one?"

"Yes," said Emily.

"Why?"

Emily widened her eyes. "Because I want a life."

"What's inside of you," said Paul, reaching out toward her stomach, "*is* a life."

"That's not what I mean, and you know it. I want to grow up and travel and meet people and—"

"Other guys?"

"Other people," said Emily. "Not just guys. But, Paul, we won't be together forever."

"Why not?"

"We just won't be. It's natural. It happens."

"Not to everybody. Your parents started dating in high school."

"Yeah," said Emily, "and yours didn't."

"You want to go to college so you can get away from me," said Paul.

"That's not true. You have nothing to do with it."

"And *that's* not true. Not anymore." He touched her stomach. "This is ours. This is us."

"No," said Emily, "this is me."

"What would your parents say if you wanted to keep it?"

"Are you kidding? They would say no way."

"Have you asked them?"

"No. What's the point? I know what they'd say."

"But it's your body," said Paul. "It's your decision."

"But they gave my body life."

"That doesn't mean they own you."

"They own me till I'm eighteen," said Emily. "That's their argument." But her parents had said no such thing.

"That's a faulty argument," said Paul.

"Yeah, to me and you it is, but——"

"Why are you taking their side?"

"I'm not!"

"Yes, you are!"

"Paul," said Emily in a quiet voice, "grow up."

Paul covered his face with his hands. "Are you breaking up with me?"

Emily waited until his hands dropped to his sides before she answered. "Yes."

"But you love me," said Paul.

"I do. But I don't want a baby."

"You don't think I'm smart enough to be a dad," he said.

"It has nothing to do with that."

"Aha! So I'm right—you don't think I'm smart."

"Paul, please." She reached for his hand, and he let her take it.

"I'm coming over to your house tonight."

"No, you're not," said Emily.

"Yes, I am. We're going to talk to them. It's awful what they're asking you to do. They might have given you life, but this is going to destroy you. I know this. I know you well enough to know that down the road—"

"Just stop. Please."

"I'm coming over," he said, squeezing her hand, "and we're going to sit down with your parents and talk. There. Is that grown-up enough for you? Is that smart enough for you?"

"Don't waste your time," said Emily. "They won't answer the door."

"I don't care," said Paul, pulling his hand away. "I'll bust open a window."

"They'll call the police."

"The police love me, remember?"

"I wish that night at Cole's house had never happened. We were stupid," said Emily. Then she handed him the letter, and when Paul opened it and saw what was there—what he already knew—he lifted his head and screamed at the sky, and then he tried to hand the paper back.

"Why did you even need to write it all down if you knew you were going to tell me in person?"

"In case you weren't here—"

"You mean that if I hadn't been home, you would have broken up with me in a *letter*?"

Paul waved the stationery in her face, but Emily refused to take it. "You know what?" she said. "This wouldn't be happening if you'd worn a condom."

He stuffed the letter in his back pocket and grabbed her by the shoulders. Emily lost her footing, falling backward into leaves that had once been gold.

"Oh, so it's my fault!" he yelled down at her.

"No, it's *our* fault!"

"Wrong! It's *your* fault!"

"How is it *my* fault?"

Paul's gray eyes turned to steel. "You could have just given me a blow job. You know that, Emily? How easy life would be if you'd just done it."

Emily let herself drop back onto the leaves. Even if Paul hadn't pushed her, she would have ended up flat on the ground. It was true: if she'd done what Paul wanted, she would be a free girl. But now she was bound to her body.

"You would never say that if you loved me," said Emily, lifting herself up. "You don't love me. You really don't."

Paul looked down at a rock and jabbed at it with the toe of his work boot before he picked it up and tossed it up and down, measuring the weight of it. He was going to throw the rock at her; Emily was sure of it. She scrambled to her feet and took off running to where her mom's car was parked. Paul started to follow her, then stopped at the top of the driveway. He was sobbing now, but he was still holding the rock. He waited until Emily was in the driver's seat, waited until she was watching, before he raised the rock high with both hands and brought it down full force on top of his head.

With shaking hands, Emily put the key in the ignition. Through the windshield she saw Paul crumple to the ground, palms pressed to his scalp. Then she turned the key, put the pedal to the metal, and flew home.

Now, Emily walks and does not fly. She walks a straight line through the front gates of the Amherst School for Girls. She crosses the quad to the lieberry to retrieve her coat. She halfway expects an army of adults to be circled around the carrel where she was sitting two hours ago, but all she finds is a note pinned to it, dashed off in slanted cursive on school stationery. *Emily Beam, Please report ASAP to the headmistress.*

. . .

The door to Dr. Ingold's office is wood with stained-glass panels. When Emily knocks, she isn't sure that anyone can hear, her fist no match for the door's thickness. Moments later, the door creaks open and a woman emerges. It is not Dr. Ingold, whom Emily met on the day she moved in, but a younger version of her, a lean woman in a white blouse and a gray skirt who introduces herself as Ms. Ledbetter, Dr. Ingold's assistant.

"Dr. Ingold will be glad to hear that you're safe," says Ms. Ledbetter, gesturing toward a chair covered in velvet. "Please. Sit. She's on the telephone. I'll let her know you're here."

Emily has waited on the other side of closed doors before. Like on that Saturday night when she should have been at Frank's Tuscan Villa celebrating her birthday. All the way up in her room, Emily heard Paul's truck screech to a halt in front of the house at seven o'clock, three hours after she had last seen him. Within seconds, Paul was ringing the doorbell. She ran downstairs, skidding into the entrance hall just as her father was reaching for the doorknob.

"Don't answer it," she said.

In that instant, Emily and her father understood each other. She was asking to be protected. Even though she might protest and rebel later, he would stand by her in that way.

Her father reached for her hand and held tight while Paul pounded on the wood, rang the doorbell over and over. Emily's mother came running into the foyer and grabbed on to Emily's other hand. When Paul realized no one was going to let him in, he pressed his finger on the bell and held it there for so long that the doorbell burned itself out, the wail of a poor man's ambulance.

Dr. Ingold's office has a cuckoo clock that sings on the quarter hour. No one in Grenfell County that Emily knows of has a cuckoo clock. It reminds her of Hansel and Gretel. Just as Dr. Ingold opens the door, the bird pops out and cuckoos three times. Dr. Ingold shakes Emily's hand and offers her a seat in a high wooden chair that looks like it came from an old church. Emily sits, nestling deeper inside her coat. One of the windows is partway open, and she can hear the train announcing its arrival into Amherst.

Dr. Ingold searches Emily's eyes before she speaks.

"I imagine that you had a good reason for leaving campus without permission."

"I did," Emily says. "I had to find Emily Dickinson's grave."

Dr. Ingold raises one eyebrow. "Go on."

Behind Dr. Ingold's desk hangs a painting of a girl sitting on a stool by a window that overlooks the ocean. The girl leans toward the water, one foot poised to go.

"This is going to be hard to explain," Emily says. "It's like my brain has been hijacked."

"I'm intrigued," Dr. Ingold says.

"I'm intrigued, too," Emily says. "I don't know what has taken it over or where it's taking me or whether I'll ever get my real brain back."

"You know, Emily, that we're going to have to send you home if you can't live with the rules here. They weren't put in place to confine you. They were put in place to make you feel secure. To give you some boundaries to guide you, to help you choose wisely, not only now but for the rest of your life."

"Yes, ma'am."

"And they are especially necessary for a girl who has so much to sort through."

Emily looks out the window at the shuddering limbs of a maple.

"Tell me, do you like your classes?"

"I do," Emily says. "Well, except for math."

"What's the problem with math?"

"Mrs. Frame is a good teacher. It's just that the subject is, I don't know . . ."

Dr. Ingold waits for her to finish the sentence, but she can't.

"How are you and K.T. Montgomery getting along?"

"She's nice," says Emily. "I like her a lot."

Dr. Ingold scribbles something on the pad of paper in front of her. "As you know, Emily, we all want it to work out for you here. I am well aware that you failed to report for a Sunday dinner last month. K.T. was terribly worried."

"Yes, ma'am."

"So I'm going to campus you for a week, starting now. That means no leaving the campus until next Wednesday, the twenty-second. And if you break another major rule, we'll have to call your parents and discuss whether ASG is the best fit for you."

Emily nods.

"Do you understand, Emily? Are we clear?"

"Yes, ma'am."

"I'll explain to Madame Colche what lured you away from French, and I'll let Mrs. Frame know why you weren't in class—again. I'm sure she'll be happy to hear that this time, you didn't lock yourself away in a water closet." Dr. Ingold offers Emily a small smile from the left corner of her mouth. "It's almost time for afternoon athletics, so I'll excuse you to go to your room to change clothes."

"Thank you," Emily says, rising from her tall chair, which, she realizes now, was chosen to make the girl sitting in it feel small.

"A letter arrived for you today," Dr. Ingold says. "The sender wasn't aware of your box number, so it ended up in our office." She lifts an envelope from her desk and hands it to Emily, who recognizes the handwriting immediately.

Dr. Ingold watches her. "Did you know that Emily Dickinson had hair almost the exact color as yours?"

"No," Emily says, touching the windblown strands of auburn that have escaped from her ponytail. "The photograph of her—"

"The daguerreotype, you mean. Photography had yet to be invented."

"The daguerreotype. It makes her hair look black."

"Our mutual friend wasn't nearly as dark as people have made her out to be. She spent hours in her garden. It was her favorite place. Remember that, please."

"I will," Emily says.

"I'm here—all of us are—if you need us."

This should be the motto that goes on all of the ASG brochures: "We're here if you need us." If Emily had a dollar for every time someone has said that to her, she could buy out the drugstore's entire supply of greeting cards and replace them with her own unsentimental, Dickinson-like sentiments.

DNA

I spend my days at Boarding School
Steeling up my spine,
Keeping faith but in myself
And books that draw the line

Between the world of spirit &
The world of proven fact,
Truths that I can measure &
Depend on to exact

The finest points of being what
God set me up to be:
A genetic composition of
Irrationality.

Emily Beam, *March 15, 1995*

BECAUSE SHE CAN'T GO FOR HER EVENING WALK, EMILY TRAVELS straight from the dining room to the lieberry with a bag full of books, a head full of thoughts, and the still-unopened letter from Ms. Albright. She wants a cigarette, but she does not want to see K.T., who ratted on her about missing Sunday dinner. No wonder K.T.'s favorite childhood book was *Harriet the Spy.*

Emily Dickinson's roommate at Mt. Holyoke Female Seminary was a spy, too. That spy wrote letters to friends at home reporting on the heathen Emily, a bad apple in danger of spoiling the barrel. The girls at the school were asked to keep their doors open at all times and to tell a teacher if another girl was ill. Back then, sickness could be deadly. But did doubt count as a disease? Did loneliness rank as an illness? Was a girl with sadness in her soul destined both for hell *and* dismissal?

Maybe I should just go ahead and leave, Emily Beam thinks. *Hop a train out of Amherst and wind my way back to Grenfell County and hole up in my bedroom for the next fifty years.* She opens the creamy white envelope from Ms. Albright.

> *Dear Emily,*
> *I was so sad to discover that we wouldn't be together*

for the duration. Your mother told me where you were, and I
looked it up in a reference book I have on the shelf here at
home. It sounds like such a wonderful school, and I know
you'll find opportunities there that we aren't able to offer
you here. Take advantage of those silver linings, and write
back when you have time to tell me what they are.

Fondly, Ms. Albright.

P.S. Please tell Emily D. I said hello. I'm sure something
of her lingers there.

Emily grabs for her throat, unable for a moment to breathe. She tears off her coat, unlaces her boots, and, in a flash of anger, throws one across the lieberry just as Amber Atkins peeks around the corner of a bookshelf. Another spy? Emily rises from her carrel and heads over to where she saw Amber lower herself into the stacks, but no one is there. Emily walks downstairs to the water fountain in her socks and takes a long drink. When she returns to her desk, K.T. is sitting at it.

"I've been looking for you," K.T. says.

"Well, you found me," says Emily.

"What happened?"

Emily looks down at her feet. "I don't want to wear shoes anymore," she says. "None of them fit."

"Listen, Emily. I had to tell Dr. Ingold. When you didn't show up for dinner that Sunday, I thought, well, honestly, I was afraid you'd gone off and hurt yourself. I know it's crazy now, but at the time, it seemed like a very real possibility. You stayed home from the St. Mark's dance that Saturday night. You asked me for matches. I had this horrible image of you setting yourself on fire." K.T. pauses. "You cry out in your sleep."

"I do?"

"At least once a night. I know something bad has happened to you, and maybe I even have an idea of what it was from reading your poems—"

"I wish I'd never showed those to you."

"I'm glad you did."

"That's what I wanted to burn—my notebook, not my body."

K.T.'s chin quivers, and she swallows before she speaks. "A good friend from home committed suicide two years ago. That's why I go to school here and not in Vermont."

Emily steadies herself on the side of the carrel. "I wish you'd told me that," she says. "I wish you'd told me the first hour I got here."

"Why? What have you ever told me?"

"I told you a lot! I told you with my poems!"

"I'd rather you tell me to my face. Look, I'll see you later, okay?"

"Sure." Emily watches K.T. leave. She gathers the boots and slowly, very slowly, puts them back on her feet.

ABSINTHE
inspired by the Edgar Degas painting, c. 1875–1876

In a café in Paris
a woman sags
to the limelight
of loss. But what
went missing
what got tossed
to the gutter?
Not her blouse
of spilled ruffles
not the prick of a pearl
or predator hat.
Even her shadow
has glued itself
to her absence.
To the gravitas
lure of her absinthe.
To absinthe.
A man wants
to pin her
to canvas blank
as the night.
But she's limped
there already
slippers tight
and all wrong.
A girl looking deep
should find the one
who's long gone.

Emily Beam, *March 15, 1995*

THE TELEPHONE ON THE SECOND FLOOR OF HART HALL RINGS JUST after ten. Annabelle Wycoff answers. When the girl on the other end of the line asks for Emily Beam, Annabelle tells her that Emily is in the library. Annabelle also shares her concern for Emily, their resident orphan. The girl on the phone tells Annabelle that she must be mistaken. Emily's mom and dad are fine—she saw them at church on Sunday.

When Emily arrives at the top of the stairs, Annabelle is waiting for her, holding the receiver out as if it were a fish she'd just caught. "Phone call, Emily."

"Who is it?"

"I knew your parents didn't ski," says Annabelle.

Emily puts the phone up to her ear. "Mom?" But she knows it isn't her mother, or Aunt Cindy; she talked to both of them on Sunday afternoon.

"Hey, Emily," says Carey. "Is this a bad time?"

Annabelle crosses her arms and plants herself, looking like the troll who guarded the billy-goat bridge.

Emily turns away and talks quietly into the phone. "Hey, I'm sorry I haven't called you back. There just aren't enough phones for all of us girls, I guess."

"Your friend said you were in the library."

"Yeah," says Emily. "I study there."

"I haven't been back in the one at school yet. Mr. Burton invited me to come and have a look around when no one else was in there, but I didn't want to."

"I don't blame you."

"They cleaned everything up, of course."

"Of course."

"I'm sure it looks just the same as it always has," Carey says, "but it won't feel the same, to be in there."

Emily gets it. The library would no longer smell like the inside of books. It would smell like disinfectant and Band-Aids.

Annabelle gives her a little wave, and Emily waves back with her middle finger. To Carey she says, "Go ahead. I'm listening."

Carey talks on as girls travel to and from the bathroom. Just as K.T. emerges from the stairwell and Waverley comes out of the room, Annabelle announces what she has learned: "The orphan story was bullshit."

Emily gives K.T. a pleading look.

"Emily?" Carey asks. "Are you there?"

Annabelle takes a step toward K.T. and says, "You owe me an explanation, Keller True Montgomery."

"I don't owe you a damn thing," K.T. says. "Because you were so obviously desperate for some drama in your life, you took what I said seriously. It was a joke, Annabelle. I can't believe you fell for it."

"All right," says Annabelle, backing up a little. "Okay."

"I don't owe you shit, not after what you did to Hannah."

"Waverley started it," Annabelle says.

154

"She's right," Waverley says. "I did."

"But you finished it, K.T.," Annabelle says. "Remember? If you hadn't ratted, Ho-Bag Hannah would still be here."

"Damn straight," says Waverley.

"It wasn't like that," says K.T., "and you know it."

"You are such a liar," Annabelle says. "No wonder you don't have any friends."

"Emily?" Carey says again. "Emily?"

Déjà vu, Emily thinks. *Déjà vu all over again.*

As soon as Paul went screeching out of her driveway in his truck, she knew she had made an irreversible error. When the phone rang a half hour later, Mr. Beam answered. He refused to let Emily talk to Paul, even though she tugged on his arm and cried and begged. He laid into Paul for ruining his daughter's life.

After her parents had gone to bed, Emily slipped downstairs, picked up the phone in the kitchen, and dialed the Wagoners' number.

Carey, not Paul, answered. "Happy birthday, Emily."

"I wish," said Emily. "Can I talk to Paul, please?"

"He's locked in his room, and he won't come out. My parents just went to bed. What happened?"

For a whole minute, Emily didn't say anything. She kept picturing the letter in the back pocket of Paul's jeans. Carey stayed on the line, and Emily put her hand over the tiny holes in the phone in case Mr. or Mrs. Wagoner picked up. Neither one of them did. The silence ticked away. Emily could hear Carey put down the phone, and in another minute, Paul said her name.

"Emily."

"Paul."

"Thanks, Carey," Paul whispered. "I've got it now." He waited for a second before he spoke. "Why? Why wouldn't you let me in?"

"It was my dad," Emily lied. "He's such an asshole." A light flipped on in the foyer. "Oh, shit," she said. "Someone's coming." It was her mother; she could tell by the slide of her slippers.

"I wanted to talk to them in person," said Paul. "I wanted to ask you this, and them, too, so I'll just say it now. Let's get married."

Emily could hear the smile in Paul's voice as her mother walked into view. In her thin nightgown, with the light behind her, Emily could see right through her. She was wearing granny underwear, and her breasts sagged.

"Tell him goodbye," said Mrs. Beam. "Hang up right now, or I'll go get your father."

"I've got to go," she told Paul. "I'll see you Monday at school, okay?"

"Yeah," said Paul, and he hung up.

For most of Sunday morning, Emily lay in bed, thinking about Paul, wondering how well she knew him. Her mom and dad decided not to go to church, and Emily wasn't sure if it was because they didn't want to run into the Wagoners or because they wanted to keep an eye on her. Just before eleven, her mom left for the grocery store, and her dad came in from the garage, where he'd been changing the oil in his car. Emily listened for him to get in the shower and called Paul's house, but no one answered.

All day, she waited for an opportunity to try again, but there wasn't one. Sunday afternoon, it snowed for a while, but all that was left on the ground early Monday morning was the dust of it, not nearly enough to cancel school. The alarm clock sounded at 6:15 a.m. like always, and Emily got herself ready to catch the bus.

She hears Carey's voice. "If you're still there, Emily, say something."

A huddle of girls has formed outside the bathroom door, watching, listening. It is wrong, but she can't help it: Emily hangs up the phone.

K.T. and Annabelle are in full face-off mode. Because K.T. is so much taller, it makes Annabelle look even more like a troll.

"Just because I'm not friends with you," K.T. is saying, "doesn't mean I don't have any friends. I choose my friends carefully; they have to be people I can trust. Emily Beam is my friend, and she had nothing to do with it. I roped her into the story. And she has nothing to do with Hannah, either, so leave Emily out of it. You bullied Hannah. I saw the notes. It was no secret to Hannah who was behind them. Who the hell are you to tell another girl what to do with her body?"

"Come on, Annabelle," Waverley says. "Let's go."

"I might not have loved Hannah every minute of every day," says K.T., "but at least I treated her like a person. You treated her like a dog."

Annabelle turns to Emily. "You'd better watch out," she says. "I wouldn't trust your dear ol' roomie for a second. Oh, and, by the way, I'm really glad you're not an orphan."

Waverley grabs Annabelle's arm and escorts her into their room. The door slams shut, and the girls in the hall disperse.

K.T. looks at Emily. "I went to Dr. Ingold because I was worried about Hannah. Just the same as I was with you. We girls are so good at hiding our pain." K.T. picks up her book bag and cello case and walks down the hall to Room 15, leaving Emily alone.

THE DOCTOR

The doctor was a woman.
She wore a smock of white.
And in the glow of evening,
she prayed with all her might.

She prayed for little children.
She prayed for all the land,
and for an angel not yet born,
tiny as a hand.

Emily Beam, *March 15, 1995*

THERE'S NO SLEEPING WEDNESDAY NIGHT. EMILY'S HEAD HAS NEVER spun like this. All in one day she has been campused, exposed, possessed, waylaid, betrayed, vilified, protected, defended, and extraordinarily productive, poetry-wise.

And what to do about Carey, who is going to therapy and wants to tell Emily something? For some reason, Emily is more scared of her than of anyone.

Emily has been to therapy, in Boston, only her parents called it "counseling." The man's name was Dr. Ferris. "Like the wheel," he said as he held out his clammy hand. Three times during the first week of the new year, Emily took the Boston subway, called "the T," from her Aunt Cindy's house in Belmont. The only way that Emily agreed to meet with Dr. Ferris was if she could go alone. She liked looking at the map of the public transportation system and figuring out how to get places she'd never been. Emily pretended she liked Dr. Ferris just so she could ride the T, which was crowded with faces she would never see again. It made her feel significant, important. For the first time, she looked forward to being an adult.

Dr. Ferris charged an outrageous amount to listen to Emily. Therapy was a complete waste all around because everything Emily told Dr. Ferris was a lie. She didn't care. Her parents were acting—everyone was acting—like something was wrong with her, when it was Paul who was messed up in the head. She had made a mistake. That was part of it, wasn't it? Make your mistakes while you're young lest you ruin the world when you're older.

"Baby steps," said Dr. Ferris. "For a while, and in some situations, you're going to feel as if you're just now learning to walk. Does that make sense?"

"Not at all," said Emily.

"It will be the same you, but there will be more *to* you— more weight, because of what you have been through—and so your legs might teeter for a while until they find a way to balance themselves."

"My legs are fine," said Emily.

"So," said Dr. Ferris, "how are you feeling?"

"I'm feeling young. I'm feeling in charge of my life. I'm feeling like a brand-new girl."

Dr. Ferris widened his eyes and nodded. "Tell me more."

God, thought Emily, *what a moron. How do you think I feel? I feel hollowed out, damned, caught in the middle of Wrong and Wronger.* Emily wanted to laugh at the stupid smile on Dr. Ferris's fat face. "Feelings pile on top of me like blankets," she said.

"That's an eloquent way of putting it," Dr. Ferris said. "Keep going."

"Well, let's see. I had no idea my boyfriend was going to kill himself, if that's what you're asking."

"That's not what I'm asking," said Dr. Ferris. "I'm not asking anything."

Emily looked at the clock. "You're trying to get me to say that it's my fault Paul killed himself," she said. "But I didn't have that kind of power over Paul. He didn't love me."

"Was that how it was between the two of you, a fight for control over the other?"

Emily stared at him with her mouth open. "We didn't sit around analyzing our relationship. We just lived, Dr. Ferris. You know, like teenagers do."

"What we're working toward here, Emily, is getting you out of the thicket of your confusion. That's my job, you see, to try to get you to a place where you've gained a little perspective. Now. Tell me how Paul reacted when you told him you were pregnant."

"He was actually very happy," Emily said. "We were riding in his truck when I told him, and he pulled over to the side of the road and got out and jumped up and down."

"Was that a reaction that you expected?"

"Yeah, pretty much."

"Would you like to tell me a little more about that?"

"No," said Emily. "I wouldn't."

She sat there with her arms crossed while Dr. Ferris studied her.

"Then let's talk about your experience at the doctor's office, shall we?"

Emily lied about that, too.

The doctor they'd used was a woman, a friend of a friend of Aunt Cindy's. On December 21, nine days after Paul died, Aunt Cindy drove Emily and her mother into the city early in the morning. The appointment was at 9:15 a.m. On the way to the doctor's office, it started to snow, and Emily thought of Paul under the ground and cried quietly into the sleeve of her coat. She could not believe she hadn't thought of it before. Paul, the last alive part of him, was inside of her. Emily put her free hand on her stomach and swallowed. "Stop," she said from the backseat. "Stop the car."

"What's wrong, honey?" her mother said, turning. "Are you okay?"

Aunt Cindy eased the car to the shoulder.

"I don't think I can do this," Emily said through her tears. "It's not right."

"Emily," her mother said. "We've made our decision, and it *is* right."

"It's the right thing for *you*," Aunt Cindy added.

"How can you say that?" Emily said. "You don't even know me."

Mrs. Beam stretched out her hand to touch Emily's cheek, but Emily pulled back. "Of course your aunt knows you," she said. "She's known you all your life."

A truck whizzed by, and the car shook.

"I've known me all my life, too," said Emily, "and *I* don't even know me."

"Shhh," her mother said. "Shhh. The doctor will take care of everything."

"No. We owe it to Paul," Emily said. "We're bad people, to be doing this."

"We are not bad people," said her mother. "We are caring people. We are practical people."

"You have lived through a trauma," said Aunt Cindy. "You have been scarred to the core of your being. Whoever you are—whoever you discover you are—you will need time to recover. Having a baby would add years to your recovery. *And* your discovery. Years."

"Think on this," said her mother. "What if you had the baby, and, when he grew up, he took a gun into his high school and threatened somebody with it? Or worse, killed somebody? Think on that, why don't you?" Mrs. Beam turned around to face forward. "The lane's clear. We can go now, Cindy."

Emily wiped her eyes and watched the flakes die, one by one, on the warm car windows. For a while, she counted them but stopped when the number got too large. What lived inside of her would die, too, on this day, like a snowflake. The only one of its kind.

CONCEPTION

She laid herself down in the velvet
of dark, the thin chirps of crickets
in the field outside the window,
the window he had opened,
the window he believed in.

When he lay down beside her,
the boy whispered truths
into the palm of her hand.
Do not leave, he said.
*Do not go. Never cut me
out; if you do, you'll feel
a sadness true as the trees.*
He kissed her lifeline
and sealed his secrets there.

Emily Beam, *March 16, 1995*

EMILY WAKES TO K.T. STANDING OVER HER, GENTLY SHAKING HER ARM.

"You cried out," K.T. says.

"What time is it?"

"Four-fifteen."

"Oh, God, K.T., I'm sorry."

"It's all right," K.T. says. "I have a big Spanish test today I haven't studied for yet anyway, and the moon is, like, blinding. It's bright as day outside. If I make some coffee, will you drink some?"

"Sure," says Emily. "I'm afraid to leave the room."

"Why?"

"Lying to a cream puff whose life's ambition is to be the leader of the free world could have in no way been a good idea."

"Aw, she's harmless. Don't worry about her."

"That's what you said last time."

"Well, this time I mean it."

"Annabelle intimidates me," Emily says. "She's got those narrow eyes and that topknot of black hair and that extra padding around her middle. She's not a pastry. She's Buddha."

K.T. laughs. In fact, she can't stop laughing, and Emily can't help but laugh, too. After she catches her breath, she says, "And Buddha was the only human to ever achieve Enlightenment, so . . ."

"You really are the bumpiest pumpkin," K.T. says.

"I probably am," says Emily, and then all of a sudden, out of nowhere, she feels her insides joining forces to say out loud what she hasn't been able to say. "I guess I have reason to be."

"What do you mean?" asks K.T.

Emily, breathing in and out, can almost smell the inside of Paul's truck. "My boyfriend killed himself."

"Oh, Emily," says K.T. "Oh, I'm sorry."

"Yeah. Me too."

"The one you told me about. Paul. The one who ran over the dog."

"Yes."

"Was Paul the one you got pregnant with?"

Emily's hand goes to her stomach. "You didn't say you knew."

"The poem about the seed, well, it seemed pretty clear. It also seemed very private."

"But I showed them to you," says Emily.

"You did," says K.T., "but I thought Madame Colche strong-armed you."

"Maybe a little."

"I can tell from the poems that you really loved him."

"I'm not so sure," Emily says. "I'm really not very sure of anything."

"You notice what other people can't see. And you feel things very deeply. I like those things about you," says K.T.

Emily and K.T. talk until the moon sets, drinking coffee. When Emily tells K.T. about what happened in the school library, she tells her all of it. As she speaks, she speaks as honestly as she knows how, and another poem finds its way into being. "Shroud," it is called, a prose poem and it goes like this:

> In the waiting room, in the clinical glow, she hugs the silence, wraps it around her shoulders, a shawl. If she'd only known, she'd have chosen its eloquence years ago, its silver thread stitching together the days. The stretch and pull of the noisy past smothers it. Music that doesn't mean. Clichéd lyrics, oppressive downbeats. Screaming that suffocates melody. How could she have been so deaf to the symphonies of silence, to the seductive absence of voice?

K.T. listens long and carefully. When Emily finishes, K.T. tells her how her friend in Vermont left a suicide note on the kitchen table with only one word on it—*love*—and went upstairs and took a bottle of her mother's sleeping pills. Now it is Emily's turn to put her arms around K.T. While she waits for the crying to ebb, Emily wonders what Dickinson would have to say. Gazing at the thick book sitting on her bedside table, Emily composes it herself.

My Words stand by as Witness
Collected and in line—
America is dying
One Girl at a Time.

· · ·

K.T. skips breakfast to study for her Spanish test, so Emily walks to the dining room alone, her toothbrush and tooth-paste tucked away in her book bag next to *The Collected Poems of Emily Dickinson.* She will use the bathroom in the lieberry to avoid running into Annabelle and Waverley. If they could find a way to get rid of Ho-Bag Hannah, then maybe they could find a way to get rid of her, too. But her darkest secret is safe, safe under the mattress and safe with K.T. Not even Dr. Ingold knows about the abortion.

· · ·

It was snowing harder when Emily and her mother emerged from the doctor's office. The snowflakes were so large they looked fake. Aunt Cindy was waiting for them two blocks away in a coffee shop. As they walked along the nearly de-serted sidewalk, Emily's mother reached more than once for Emily's hand, but the last thing Emily wanted to feel was a connection to her mother, so she stuffed her mittened hands inside the pockets of her coat.

Aunt Cindy was sitting at a table reading the newspaper and drinking coffee.

"See if there's something you'd like to drink," Aunt Cindy told Emily. "I wasn't sure what you'd want."

Emily turned and looked toward the counter. Beyond it, at the end of a narrow hall, was a door to the outside. Through its small window, Emily could see snow drifting down like a lacy veil.

"I have to go to the bathroom," she said.

"How are you feeling now, honey?" her mother asked.

"Oh, fine," said Emily. "A little groggy but fine."

"It doesn't hurt?" Aunt Cindy said.

"Not yet," Emily said.

"It won't start hurting until all the anesthesia wears off," Emily's mother explained.

"Here's some money," said Aunt Cindy, holding out a bill. "Get your mom a cup of coffee, and get yourself something, too, okay? Whatever looks good to you."

"Thanks," said Emily. She walked past the counter and down the hall. At the door of the bathroom, she turned and looked back at the two women at the table, their heads leaning into one another's. In one swift move, Emily sidestepped out the back door of the shop and into the falling snow. Across the street was a stop for the T. She hurried over. With the five dollars Aunt Cindy had given her, she bought a ticket and took the red-line train to Harvard because it was the only name on the map inside the station that she recognized.

Emily had no idea what to do once she got there, and she didn't care. She was living in the moment—not in the past, not in the future. How or when she would get back to Aunt Cindy's house didn't matter because what mattered was now, right now, and right now, Emily wanted to be someone else.

When she emerged from underground, she walked through the Harvard campus in the falling snow, pretending to be a student, although there weren't many of them around. Because the sanitary pad was bulky and her stomach was starting to cramp, Emily stopped into a deli near campus and sat down at a table by the window. When, after ten minutes, no one came to take her order, she realized she was supposed to tell the man at the counter what she wanted. She walked up and ordered a bagel with butter and a cup of coffee. "Pretty lady, numbah fifty-two," the man said in his rich Boston accent. Even though her stomach hurt, she smiled. It felt exquisite, being anonymous. Fifty-two would be her lucky number forever. It was her first cup of coffee, and though she took only two bites of the bagel, it was the best meal she'd eaten in her life.

The coffee and bagel she has for breakfast this morning at ASG are good, too, but they can't compete. Emily Beam is known here. She has a past, but she also has a future, dangling like a carrot on the end of a string. If she ever reaches it, if she ever gets to take a bite, then it will no longer be the future. In the moment of tasting, it becomes the present, and in the time that it takes to swallow, it is past. Time, both friend and enemy, confounds her.

As she rises to leave the dining room, Amber Atkins approaches.

"Hey, Emily. You want to study for the French test with me?"

"Maybe tonight after dinner."

"Okay," says Amber, "but I kind of need to tell you something now."

"Then tell me."

"I need to tell you in private."

Emily looks around. No one is listening. No one is even watching. All over the dining room, girls are in the middle of living.

Amber whispers, "I took something."

"Let me guess. A lipstick."

"No, not lipstick. Something else. Something bigger."

"What does this have to do with me?"

"Because you were there," says Amber.

"Where?"

"At Emily Dickinson's house."

"Oh. So you were the one who put the crocus in my carrel."

Amber winks.

"Look, Amber, I don't think stealing a flower is a big deal. Plus, that was, like, a month ago."

"I'm not talking about the crocus. Follow me." Amber leads Emily out onto the quad and across to the lieberry, where Amber makes a beeline for the bathroom.

"Hello?" she calls. "Anyone here?" She checks under the stalls and opens one of the doors. "Get in," she tells Emily.

"What?"

"No one can see this."

"You're freaking me out, Amber."

"Don't flatter yourself." Amber swings the stall door closed and slides the lock into place before she unzips her backpack and pulls out a long white dress.

"Holy shit," Emily says.

"I found it last night. Behind the house."

"You stole it."

"I swear I didn't. I was just out walking, you know, like we do sometimes, and I found it in the garden."

"Do you know whose dress that is?"

"I do now," says Amber.

Emily reaches out to brush her hand over the pocket. "Can I touch it?"

"Sure."

Amber passes her the dress, which Emily holds up in front of her. It's thin, cotton, long-sleeved, with a neat collar and delicate mother-of-pearl buttons down the front all the way past the knee. At the right hip, there is an oversized, hand-stitched pocket.

"What are you going to do with the dress?"

"Take it back, of course!"

"How did it end up in the yard?"

"How the hell should I know? I was just walking by and—voila!—there it was."

"It should be in the house," says Emily.

"I know that," says Amber.

"They keep it on display in her room."

"I know!"

"So how are you going to get it back there?" Emily asks. "Because if you don't, guess what?"

"It'll look like I took it."

"Exactly."

"That's why I came to you," says Amber. "You're the poet around here. Couldn't you, like, sweet-talk your way in and put it back?"

"Are you crazy?"

"Yeah, probably. My mom thinks so."

Emily pictures the sign by the front gate of the house: *Open Saturdays & Sundays 12–5.* "The house is going to open back up again in two days."

"That's why I need you to sweet-talk your way in there before then."

"Not gonna happen," says Emily. "The last thing I need right now is to get into more trouble."

"What kind of trouble are you in?"

"Never mind."

"It can't be as much trouble as I'm in," says Amber. "I've got, like, fifty Hashes. I, like, *live* in Detention Hall."

"Well, I'm campused."

"Till when?"

"Next Wednesday," Emily says. "And I am not leaving campus till then."

Gently, Emily reaches her hand inside the dress and lifts out a scrap of paper, brittle and yellow and torn.

"Did you put this in here?" she asks Amber.

"No."

"Swear it," says Emily.

"Don't you believe anything?"

"Not anything *you* say."

Amber sighs. "I swear on my mother's fat ass—sorry, Mom, but it's true—that I did not put that piece of paper in that pocket." When she leans in to see what it says, Emily jerks her hand away.

"What does the piece of paper say?"

"Nope," says Emily, "not until you promise to leave me alone about all this. I don't want to get kicked out. I like it here."

"But Madame Colche says you're a genius. And geniuses can figure things out, like how to get missing dresses back inside locked houses."

"You're a genius, too."

"Yeah," Amber says, "but I'm on Strike Three Probation."

"For what?"

"What do you think?"

Emily rolls her eyes.

"I didn't steal the dress, Emily! It was just, like, lying there on the grass in the moonlight. I thought it was a dead person. It scared the crap out of me."

"Then put it back in the yard where you found it. If you didn't take it, then no big deal, right?"

Amber shakes her head.

"So what did you steal? At school, I mean."

"Somebody's Diet Coke out of the fridge and a couple of cookies from my roommate's care package." Amber shrugs. "I couldn't help it. I missed dinner that night, and I was starving."

Emily unlocks the stall door. "I've got to go to class."

"Don't tell anybody," Amber says.

"I'm not stupid."

"That's right. You're a genius. Please, Emily. Please? I'm terrified of naked mannequins, especially that one."

"Aha! So you *were* in that room! How else would you know about the mannequin, huh, Amber? Not to mention the fact that the naked part was all your doing. Stop lying. Just stop."

"All right, yeah, I was there." Amber pointed at the scrap of paper. "Aren't you going to give that back?"

"Nope."

Emily walks to English pressing the scrap of paper flat to her palm. *An unexpected Maid,* it reads in faded black ink. All through English, while she is supposed to be revising an essay on "The Road Not Taken," Emily scans the collection of Dickinson poems, looking for the line and the poem it belongs to.

All through Chemistry, while she is supposed to be solving problems of spontaneous reactions, Emily searches. She finds the line at the beginning of the book in a poem she missed the first time through. Emily makes it appear that she's really into the endothermic and exothermic properties of chemical reactions, but she's not—she's contemplating Poem 17.

> *Baffled for just a day or two—*
> *Embarrassed—not afraid—*
> *Encounter in my garden*
> *An unexpected Maid.*
> *She beckons, and the woods start—*
> *She nods, and all begin—*
> *Surely, such a country*
> *I was never in!*

Who is the maid? A particularly beautiful flower? Springtime? But what is embarrassing about the spring? If the maid is a person, she is not a servant-maid. She is not a virgin overtaken by a man. No, this maid has the power.

At lunch, Emily goes back to her room, writes two poems, and sleeps until French, where she ignores Amber Atkins and pays attention to Madame Colche, wholly and devoutly, like she's supposed to.

ANTHOLOGY

What binds together the moments
of earthly grace? What gathers up
the last white daisy in an amber field;
a baby bird hatching from a speckled egg;
the look in a teacher's kind eyes,
a look that says, *You are gifted*?
Gifted as in *given by God,*
like the words she penned on cold
winter mornings so that
someone way down the way,
someone far into history,
might know what it felt like to be
what she had become: a girl
whose life was an anthology
of sad.

Emily Beam, *March 16, 1995*

HOLD UP

I can tell by your dimestore walk
you want it back:
your meadow-clear mind
your blank page
your hours and days unwasted
your childhood
your heart untorn
and just doing
its hearty job pumping
your blood
an organ
not risen up from the swamp
of evolution merely to be
twisted out of your body
by a manicured fist
and left to hang by a sinew
from your sleeve
The worst part is—
whatever she took
you let her have it
So, my brother, go
and let her have it
after you hold up
your palm and give me five
five dollars five quarters five minutes
five lifetimes five gallons of the blood
you are out for

Emily Beam, *March 16, 1995*

SOMETIMES, LIKE NOW, AS SHE'S RUNNING AROUND THE DIRT TRACK during Fitness for Fun, the sound of a thousand bells—doorbells, alarm bells, school bells, church bells, sleigh bells—rings in Emily's ears. She can make them play symphonies; she can make them play hymns: "O God, Our Help in Ages Past." She can make the bells peal out short little poems, the downbeats in sync with her footfalls:

> Staying power is gradual.
> We feel it through the soul,
> The poetry that happens when
> New Eyes see like Old!

On December 12, Paul walked down the hall to the library, believing deeply in life, in the power of youth, wanting for Emily to believe in those things, too. And she didn't, not at the time, not with the fervency that he did. In the dust under her running feet, there is a message that she couldn't hear then: *life, life, life.*

. . .

On Thursday night, as soon as dinner is over, Emily falls into a deep sleep while K.T. listens to classical music and plays the air-cello. Madame Colche drops by—Amber does, too—but even though she tries, Emily cannot wake up. The cups of coffee she drank in place of dessert can't keep up with her need for sleep. In one dream, a white cloud floats toward her in a sunlit field and hovers, delivering paper snowflakes with lines from poems written on them. When she wakes Friday morning, she can still remember some of the phrases, but it's 7:45, so she has only enough time to rush into the bathroom and chug down a cup of K.T.'s home brew before class begins.

When Emily told K.T. about that snowy day in Boston, she admitted that she stole the Harvard sweatshirt from the campus bookstore, walked straight out with it on under her coat. She got back to Aunt Cindy's house in Belmont by taking the red-line T to the end of the line. Yes, her mother yelled at her and punished her with therapy and grounded her for the rest of their time in Boston, but where was she going to go? That kind of grounded was nothing compared to the kind of grounded she felt sitting in the recovery room with two other girls, waiting for the better part of the anesthesia to wear off. For K.T., Emily assessed it as a snapshot, a single image, like a parody of a brochure for a private girls' school: one white girl, one black girl, and one Latino girl, all colors of the rainbow represented, slumped in chairs, the useless blood trickling out of them.

"Did you talk to each other?" K.T. asked.

"No," Emily said. "We should have, though."

"Why didn't you?"

Emily thought for a moment. "Because the voices in our heads had already started up."

MOSAICS

In childhood, they had killed things:
ants, bees, a bird, a squirrel, a dog.
Accidents, mostly all
accidents. They could have

dealt with it inside the fog
of memory. If time were kind—
as time is known to be—they could
trick their hearts into telling

another tale, a believable one
about a boy and a girl
with magical days laid out
like mosaics.

The tiles of their past
rearranged, redefined.

Emily Beam, *March 17, 1995*

FRIDAY NIGHT, BEFORE SHE FALLS ASLEEP, EMILY READS THROUGH THE poems in her notebook. In the nine weeks that she's been here, she's completed twenty-seven, plus twice that many fragments and half-finished poems and, of course, there's the hidden one under her mattress that she wrote eighteen days ago, which now feels like eighteen hundred days.

When Emily Dickinson died, her younger sister, Lavinia, burned all of her correspondence, as Emily had requested. But Vinnie, as Emily called her, was stunned to discover among her sister's papers nearly two thousand poems bundled into booklets. All those years of living in the house together, and Emily had kept them to herself. Vinnie read the poems. She thought they deserved an audience, and so she took it upon herself to get her sister's work published.

Emily Beam isn't sure how to feel about Vinnie's decision. On the one hand, she is grateful, because otherwise, she would never have heard of Emily Dickinson. On the other hand, here she is, with her own private stash of poems not meant for anyone's eyes, though other eyes have seen them. She finds the folded-up flyer at the back of her notebook, the one announcing the poetry contest. With her black pen, Emily puts Xs through all of the blanks on the entry form. She marks through the contest deadline—Monday, March 20— and scratches all the way across the paper, like a six-year-old who's just learned to spell his first bad word, *POETRY SUCKS!!!!!!!!!!!!!!!!!!!!!!!* After she balls up the paper and throws it in the trash can, she lies flat on her back and falls asleep, exclamation points rolling through her brain on little wheels.

On Saturday morning she wakes with numb lips. In a dream, she has been kissing Paul under a scratchy blanket in a cold, abandoned barn. K.T. is in the bathroom, where Emily will have to go in a minute. So far, she has avoided conversation with Annabelle and Waverley, though she has passed them in the hall and smiled a fake smile, which they return with their own fake smiles. In the dim light, when Emily reaches into the top drawer of her dresser for a clean pair of underwear, her fingertips meet an unexpected fabric. Emily pulls out the white cotton dress just as K.T. kicks open the door with her foot. Emily tucks the dress behind her.

"I wish we could go for a walk today," K.T. says. "I'd like to see that eagle again."

When K.T. isn't looking, Emily stuffs the dress back in the drawer.

"Yeah, me too," says Emily.

"If you get lonely this afternoon, come visit. I'll be in the music room practicing. Vivaldi is kicking my ass." K.T. wraps her wet blond hair up into a topknot. "Blond Buddha."

Emily laughs. "Hey, I'm skipping breakfast this morning. You were right about the coffee in the dining room. It *is* full of dreams."

. . .

Emily finishes her test on chemical reactions later that morning with minutes to spare. Carefully, she reaches into her book bag so as not to disturb the dress that is wrapped in the Harvard sweatshirt and fishes around for the book of Dickinson poems. She opens it to Poem 17, but the metaphor is too ambiguous. She does not know, either, what to do with the dress. French doesn't meet on Saturday mornings, and Amber isn't in her room in Sweetser Hall when Emily goes looking for her after U.S. History, the last class of the day. When Emily unzips her book bag, a sleeve of the dress flutters out of the sweatshirt and into the sudden light like a kaleidoscope of butterflies, and she has to zip it back again. She walks to the security desk in the administration building and checks the sign-out sheet for Amber's name, but it's not there.

On her way back to 15 Hart Hall, Emily notices that Madame Colche's porch light is still on from the night before. As she's looking at it, the light winks at her. Three times. Emily walks across the quad and knocks on the door.

"I need a favor," Emily says when Madame Colche opens it.

"Come in, dear."

Madame Colche gestures to a chair in the parlor, and Emily sits.

"I'm campused till Wednesday, as you know. But, if it's at all possible, I really need to tour the Emily Dickinson House before then. I know you're a member of the Society, so I thought, well, that you might be able to help me out."

"Can you explain to me the sense of urgency? The house

has stood for one hundred fifty years. Surely it can last another few days. And you've been here for how many now?"

"Sixty-three."

"En français, s'il vous plaît."

Emily thinks for a second. *"Soixante-trois."* She takes a deep breath. "I'm working on a poem for the contest. It's about Emily Dickinson writing a poem, and I want to see the place, the exact spot, where she wrote."

"I see."

"The idea just came to me last night, and the contest deadline is Monday, so . . ."

"Isn't there a photograph of Emily's bedroom in the book I gave you?"

"Yes, ma'am."

"And also a close-up of the desk where she wrote most of her poems, if I'm not mistaken. Do you not think, under the circumstances, that these will suffice?"

"I'll know what it looks like," says Emily, "but I won't know what it *feels* like. And feelings are the most important things."

"Being campused is a serious punishment. I doubt that in this case, Dr. Ingold will be sympathetic to the superiority of feeling over fact. Now, on Wednesday, when you are free to roam about, I'll be more than happy to take you on a private tour of the house."

"That would be very nice," Emily says.

"En français, s'il vous plaît, Mademoiselle Beam."

"Ça serait gentil."

"Très bon!" says Madame Colche, hopping up with a clap of her hands. *"C'est un beau samedi, n'est-ce pas?"*

"Yes," says Emily in English, rising from her chair. "Yes, it's a beautiful Saturday."

Outside, the sun has come out, and as Madame Colche closes her front door, Emily wishes she were on the bench across from the big yellow house at 280 Main Street, soaking up the early spring. Her stomach is growling, so she heads to the dining room.

After she gets her tray, she looks around for Amber. K.T. is sitting with the members of the string quartet, and she waves Emily over.

"I think you all know each other," K.T. says. The girls and Emily exchange their hellos.

"How's Vivaldi?" Emily asks. "Is it *The Four Seasons* that you're working on?"

Ms. Albright had played the class a CD of Vivaldi's *The Four Seasons*. Before she met K.T., it was the only piece of classical music Emily could name other than *The Nutcracker* and *Swan Lake*.

"Yes, and 'Winter' is a bitch," says Lucy, a violinist.

Emily laughs. "I'm ready for spring, too."

"Only three days away," K.T. says.

"For now we have to drink our warmth," says Jillian, the other violinist, rising from the table. "Anyone want more coffee?"

. . .

After lunch, Emily finds a bench in the quad and turns her face to the sun, but the spot does not offer the same delicious feeling as the bench on Main Street. With her book bag still in tow, Emily walks across the lawn to the edge of campus. The stone wall is too high to climb, but she ducks inside a circle of tall boxwoods and reaches into the zippered pocket for a cigarette and a pack of matches.

It's time, she thinks. *Time to make something happen instead of waiting for it.* She puts the cigarette in her mouth. The breeze is light, and the cigarette ignites on the first try. She inhales and exhales slowly, wondering if meditating is something like this. Her mind begins to buzz as if full of bees. Honeybees that pollinate, bouncing from blossom to blossom. Emily Dickinson loved her bees. *We—Bee and I—live by the quaffing,* she wrote in Poem 230. So many poems with bees in them. Dr. Ingold was right; Emily Dickinson spent hours in her garden.

Could a favorite white dress find its way back to the place it loved the most? What if Amber didn't steal it? What if there really were ghosts who returned to tidy up on earth? Emily takes one last drag on the cigarette and snuffs it out on the pebbles before climbing back through the boxwoods. As if she owns the place, she walks around the lieberry and out the side gate and runs all the way to the bench on Main Street.

Empty but awash in sunlight, the bench looks happy to see her. Surely, it has been waiting; surely, it has missed her company. Emily sits and lights another cigarette. A man and woman with a baby stroller pass by and shoot her two equally dirty looks. *"Allez-vous faire foutre,"* she says, but not loudly enough for the couple to hear. "Fuck you" was the first French phrase she learned at Grenfell County High School. Not from her teacher, of course.

As she smokes, three old ladies struggle up the steps to

the Emily Dickinson House. The front door opens, and, one by one, they disappear inside. Down the street, a girl comes barreling toward her, a canvas bag bouncing at her hip.

"I am so mad at you," Emily says when Amber gets close enough to hear.

"Do you have it?" says Amber, panting.

"Yeah."

"What about the slip of paper?"

"I put it back in the pocket."

"What does it say?"

"It says, 'Amber Atkins is evil.' Don't you even care that I'm here where I shouldn't be?"

Amber laughs and sits down on the edge of the bench, dropping the large bag, full of art supplies, on the ground. "You can hate me, but you can also love me."

"What do you mean?"

"When I went to your room to find you, I caught Annabelle Wycoff leaving it."

"Was K.T. there?"

"No," Amber says, "K.T. was not there."

"Just like when you snuck in with the dress, right? What the hell? Why doesn't this school believe in locks?"

"Guess what Annabelle had in her hands?"

Emily's heart jumps into her throat as Amber bends down and opens her bag.

"Oh, my God," says Emily.

Amber holds up Emily's poetry notebook. "I recognized it. From breakfast that day. So I wrestled it out of her greedy little hands."

With one deep inhale, Emily crushes the rest of the cigarette under her boot. "I thought I put it in my book bag first thing this morning! Give me that!" She flips through it, page after page. She counts. They're all there, even the loose ones.

"You can thank me," Amber says.

"I can," says Emily, "but I won't."

Amber shakes her head. "So what's the plan?"

Emily straightens her shoulders and points to the yellow brick house across the street. "I'm going to leave it in the yard once all the people leave."

"Well, I could have done that."

"Exactly!"

Emily and Amber watch as a man photographs two smiling young women on the front porch.

"This might be tricky," Amber says.

"No shit. Right now, there are five people inside, maybe more. Plus the docents and that family wandering around in the garden."

"I think it would be easier if you went inside and, like, left it in the bedroom when no one was looking."

"What if they have a docent standing in the bedroom the whole time?" Emily asks.

"They don't need a docent when they've got that scary-ass mannequin watching your every move."

Emily stares Amber down until Amber looks away. "I want to know why you stole it. Look, I've stolen things, too, all right?"

Amber bends her head so that her hair veils her face. "I like the challenge. And I did it for you."

"For me?"

"Because you didn't tell on me about the lipstick—"

"So because I don't tell on you for almost stealing, you thank me by stealing. That makes no sense."

"No," says Amber, shaking the hair from her eyes. "What I mean is, I could tell that first night that you had lost something. Something white. And I was right because when you talked about visiting your friend in Ohio in front of the class, you blinked a lot."

"I did?"

"I was about to hand you my sunglasses, you blinked so much. I thought you were about to start bawling. Whatever it was you'd lost, I could tell you wouldn't be getting it back."

Emily scans Amber's face for a glimpse of Paul. Hadn't he said something like that once, something about loss? Hadn't he tried to blink it away?

"God, Amber," says Emily. "You really freak me out sometimes, you know that?"

Amber holds up her hands. "I'm just saying."

"Well, stop. Stop saying. Don't you have any other friends who've lost shit? What about Harriet from French or those Goth girls you sit with at lunch? There's no doubt in my mind that they're losers. And I mean that in the literal sense."

Amber tucks her hair behind her ears. "Look, Emily, I have plenty of friends. But none of them are poets. You need to be in that house. It's crazy, I know, for me to say that, but I know you need to stand for a minute in that room. There's something otherworldly in there. Call it a ghost, call it whatever you want, but it's there."

"If I go," says Emily, "will you sit here and wait for me?"

"Why do you think I brought my paints? I'm going to

do the house and give it to you as a token of my deep and abiding appreciation. And the painting shall be called—drumroll, please—*The White House.*"

"But it's yellow," says Emily.

Amber rolls her eyes. "Beam. You'll never make it as a poet if you're that literal."

. . .

By three o'clock, Emily has smoked her last two cigarettes and has walked to the drugstore in the middle of town. It's the same girl behind the counter as last time, and she hands Emily, along with a pack, three books of matches. Emily smokes another one on the way back to the bench, where Amber sits in full sun with her canvas and palette. Emily's head buzzes with nicotine and adrenaline and images of bees. The visitors to the Emily Dickinson House keep coming and going. At four-fifteen, by Emily and Amber's count, there are nine people inside and a few more wandering around in the garden.

"I don't think I'm going to be able to pull this off," Emily says. "I had no idea Emily Dickinson was so popular."

"Are you kidding?" says Amber. "That's how ASG gets half of its students—by advertising itself as the school that educated America's greatest poet. Hey, and soon they can brag that it educated America's two greatest poets."

"You didn't look in my notebook, did you?"

"I glanced at a page or two. Will you remember me when you're famous?"

"Shut up," Emily says, checking her watch. "All right. I

can't wait any longer. I'm going in." She stands and throws her book bag over her shoulder. "You'll be here, right? Just in case I get arrested?"

Amber knights Emily on the shoulder with her paintbrush. "Get thee to the White House."

Emily crosses the street and opens the iron gate. The steps to the front door are worn from over a hundred and fifty years of coming and going. Between the scrolls of two Ionic columns on the porch, a bird has built a nest. Emily opens the door, painted forest green, and hands a woman with a pouf of white hair her ASG student ID, which gets her in for free.

"Another Emily," the woman says. She has on lipstick the color of cotton candy and a sweet smile to match. She reminds Emily of Paul's grandmother. "Are you a poet, too?"

"Not really," Emily says.

"It is so lovely to see you girls taking advantage of this house," the woman says, handing her a brochure. "Now, what we offer is a self-guided tour. After you walk through the house, exit through the back door if you'd like to see Miss Emily's garden. There's a volunteer in the gift shop at the rear of the house who can point you in the right direction."

"Yes, ma'am," says Emily, eying the steps curving upward.

"You only have fifteen minutes before we close, but enjoy your visit. And don't be surprised if you see Miss Emily," the woman says with a wink. "She's been spotted before at this time of day."

The light of day's end slants through the windows of the dining room. Across the hall is a dark parlor. The curtains are drawn, and a piano announces its sad silence, photographs in frames sitting on top of it. Emily leans in to study them so as not to appear too eager to wind her way up to the poet's bedroom. She can hear voices on the stairs, footsteps coming down. An old man with a cane and a woman on his arm talk intimately with one another and then with the woman at the front door. There is a rise of laughter, then more talking. Emily takes her chance and slips upstairs.

The room down the hall is just like the pictures, neat and spare, with a small bed dressed in a clean, white coverlet. The mannequin in the corner isn't naked; it wears a brown dress with long, puffy sleeves. Emily walks over to the two windows facing the front yard. In between the giant evergreens, she can see Amber across the street on the bench. Emily turns to the desk, a simple, wooden table on elegant legs. The desk's surface is so small that there's room only for an elbow and a single sheet of paper. Just as she is lowering herself into the desk chair, the woman from downstairs appears in the doorway.

"I forgot to tell you not to sit on any of the furniture," the woman says, not unkindly. "But it's tempting, isn't it?"

Emily jerks herself up. "I'm so sorry."

"It's a sweet room. You can understand why she spent so much time in here."

Emily nods. "Is there a bathroom I can use?"

"Downstairs by the gift shop," the woman says, pointing. "You'll see it on your way out."

Emily thanks her, leaving the woman standing by the mannequin, and hurries down the cascade of steps. She finds the bathroom, turns on the light, and locks herself inside. She unzips her book bag, reaching for the sweatshirt, but it seems all wrong, to leave the dress in a room with no windows. She closes the lid of the toilet and sits down to think. After a moment, she gets up and turns the light off and sits down again.

She hears the voice of the cloud-haired woman sweep by, announcing that the house will be closing in five minutes. Emily squints at her watch. A door somewhere to her right slams; the wooden floors outside of the bathroom creak with fast steps. Keys jangle, and then another door, a nearer one, clicks closed. Emily realizes that she's been holding her breath. With a silent exhale, she thinks of Amber sitting across the street on the bench. *Let her sit,* Emily thinks. *Let her paint her weird little heart out.*

Long after the sounds of other people in the house have ceased, Emily unlocks the door. She can tell from the shadows on the Oriental rug that it is still light outside, so she makes her way (baby steps!) to the parlor and crouches down on the floor by the piano bench, away from the windows, even though the curtains are drawn. No house has ever been as quiet as this one.

Emily reaches up with her right hand and brushes her fingers across the ivory keys. Wasn't Vinnie the pianist in the family? Emily presses her index finger down, and a note trembles forth. What would Ms. Albright say? And Madame Colche, who would no doubt approve of her choice of the parlor as the place to hide out until dark. But K.T. will be worried, and Amber, too, though at least Amber knows where she is.

What would Paul say, who at one time believed that a fallen leaf just might be able to reattach itself to its mother branch? How could it be the same Paul who, a decade later in his school library, had looked at the gun in his hands as if it had fallen straight from the sky? That was part of what had frightened Emily so much—that all of a sudden, with the gun in his hands, Paul seemed to possess an alien's awareness or maybe even the secret to the universe, and in the split second before she dropped to her knees, Emily thought, *Holy shit, Paul is right, and I am wrong, and* I'm *the one who doesn't get it,* and she didn't know what to say, the right words did not come, and God was not with her, as she'd believed all her life that He would be.

For a flash of a second, she saw the Paul she had given herself to in his soft gray eyes. "I don't know what I'm doing," he said. He was crying.

"I know," said Emily. "I know."

"I meant what I said on the phone Saturday night. I want to get married. Emily, please, marry me."

With the gun in his hand, she was afraid to say no. She nodded.

"You're lying," Paul said.

Emily shifted her eyes to the book on the floor. "Yes," she whispered. "I am."

"You don't love me," said Paul. "You don't love me."

She is so ashamed of herself that she couldn't tell K.T. what she said next, but she can say it now. She speaks the words aloud, tasting them for a second awful time.

"It wouldn't be fair. To the baby, I mean. A mother and father should love one another for the baby's sake, Paul."

Pall. Pall. Pall.

Emily will hear these words forever. She *used* the life

growing inside her. She had used it to save her own skin. That was what she said, and all she said, before the silence strangled her and Ms. Albright appeared, and Paul ran away, not from Ms. Albright, who offered Paul her hand, but from Emily, who didn't.

Emily reaches up again and plays another key on the piano. *That's for you, Ms. Albright,* she thinks. *And so is this one.* She presses another key to keep the first note from fading away into the old-house smell. Emily Dickinson had grown hyacinths indoors. It wouldn't have smelled like an old house in the spring when the hyacinths bloomed. Emily unzips the book bag and lifts out the dress wrapped in the sweatshirt. Standing, she unrolls it so that it cascades in front of her. The dress is her size. Emily Dickinson was on the small side, like Emily Beam.

Emily jerks her turtleneck sweater over her head and tosses it on the floor of the now-dark parlor. She unbuttons the mother-of-pearl buttons and inches the dress over her head. As she stands there, breathing in another century, another lifetime, she is certain she is going to cry, she is sure her body will give itself over to grief, so she lifts the dress away from her head for fear she might ruin it with her tears. She puts her sweater on again and lays the dress over one shoulder, holding it in place. With her other hand, she unlaces her boots and works her feet out of them. She lifts her book bag over her other shoulder, and by feeling her way, she baby-steps up the stairs in her socks to the bedroom. The door is wide open. Through one of the windows, she can see the outline of Amber on the bench. The mannequin, blank-faced and thin-lipped, stares out at nothing, the brown skirt of the dress like a bell. In the dusk, the bodice looks as if it's made of thousands of tiny gold feathers.

When Emily was in kindergarten, she thought the moon was God's eyeball, and she told Miss Claire, who smiled and said, "Perfect. God is a Cyclops." Emily had no idea what a Cyclops was, but Miss Claire explained that it was a giant with a single eye in the middle of his face. Then Miss Claire told the class that a lot of people, moms and dads, grand-mothers and grandfathers, really and truly believed that the moon was made of cheese. Emily and her classmates sat on their little squares of carpet, agape. For many of them, and for Emily, too, it was the first time that a grown-up had treated them as equals. *Listen, good children,* Miss Claire seemed to say, *you are more sensible than the masses. Trust your thoughts.*

It was the same way when Paul first took Emily into his confidence. She had felt like a chosen one. Not another girl but a boy had picked her to tell his secrets to.

On their first date, September 9, 1994, Emily and Paul were the youngest couple at Frank's Tuscan Villa. Paul had made reservations at a corner table, and he pulled Emily's chair out for her after the hostess set the menus down. At first, they'd made small talk. Emily could tell that Paul was nervous because he asked her questions he already knew the answers to: What is your favorite subject in school? (English.) What kind of music do you like? (Shawn Colvin, Indigo Girls, stuff like that.) Do you want to go to college? (Yes, very much.) Where? (I don't know yet.) When the waiter came to take their order, Paul told Emily to order anything she'd like. She ordered eggplant parmesan, which she'd never tried before, and a house salad with blue cheese dressing, which came with the meal. Paul ordered spaghetti and meatballs with no salad.

"This is delicious," Emily said, pointing at the eggplant. "Thank you."

"You're welcome."

"I don't think I'll have room for dessert. This portion is so huge."

"You don't have to eat it all."

"Oh, but I want to," Emily said.

It wasn't easy to be on a first date eating Italian food. Emily was sure she'd end up with some of it on her light-blue sweater. Less than two minutes into the meal, Paul spilled sauce on the front of his white button-down.

That broke the ice. They laughed, and what was so fun, the most wonderful thing about the whole night, was that they talked about a lot of things Emily had never discussed with boys. Paul asked her what her favorite possession was. "My grandmother's childhood dictionary," she told him, because her grandmother, who had died when Emily was eleven, had drawn little pictures in the margins to help her remember the words. His, he said, was his driver's license.

They had talked a lot about their grandparents. Paul had a good handshake, thanks to his grandfather, Gigi's husband, who was the one who first taught Paul about the wide world of trees. On the day after Paul graduated from kindergarten, he and his grandpa had taken a long walk through the woods. His grandpa taught him how to identify trees by their leaves and their bark. Life happened in the woods, his grandpa said, and so the woods were worth knowing. He told Paul what would happen to each tree when autumn came, what color the leaves would turn and when they would fall. The red oaks didn't lose their leaves at all, and Paul decided then and there that they were his favorite.

"Mine too," his grandpa said. He reached his hand out to Paul, and when Paul shook it, his grandpa said, "Darn, boy. We've got to work on that."

"Show me," Emily said to Paul. "How to shake hands." She held out her right hand across the table, and with his own right hand, Paul gripped hers and shook once, down and up.

Come to find out, she *had* wanted dessert. Being with Paul made her hungry. He recommended the tiramisu, which they shared. On the way from Frank's back to Emily's house, Paul made a detour on a county road.

"Is it okay?" he asked. "If we park somewhere and talk some more?"

The road was lined with maples, which would have been a canopy of color had they been passing under it in the light of day. But it was dark, darker than any road Emily had ever ridden down. After a couple of miles, Paul turned left onto a gravel driveway, and the truck bounced its way up to an abandoned barn.

"There was a fire here a long time ago," Paul said.

"I hope no one died. Or any cows or horses."

"Whatever happened, it happened before we were born." Paul turned off the engine. "I have a flashlight, if you want to look around."

"No," Emily said. "Let's just sit here." She placed her left hand on the seat, and Paul reached for it.

They sat for a minute, holding hands, the wind and the leaves speaking for them through the open windows.

"Maybe it wouldn't be so bad, to die in a fire," Paul said.

"What do you mean?"

"I mean, if you wanted to be cremated anyway, you'd have nature doing the job for you. And you'd pass out from the smoke inhalation before the flames reached you and all that."

Emily shuddered. "Do you want to be cremated?" she asked.

"Yeah. Ashes to ashes. I don't believe everything the Bible says, but I believe some of it."

"Like what? What parts do you believe?"

"The Do Unto Others part, for one thing. I totally believe in that. And I believe that life is a gift given by God or some higher power. But everlasting life?" Paul shook his head. "I'm not so sure about that one."

"I'm not sure about that one, either," said Emily. "Because God didn't write the Bible. Men did, probably uneducated ones."

She had said it to make Paul laugh, but he didn't.

"I think about it, but then I have to make myself stop because it's so depressing. All of the people in the world, and the animals, too, all of the people and animals that have ever lived, all of the trees, and all of the thousands and thousands of years before us, all of that life died, and all the people we know will die, too, and all of the people who are born after us, and so there's no possible way we'll see each other again because how could we all fit up there in heaven?" He paused. "You probably think I'm crazy."

"No," Emily said. "No, I don't."

"Really?"

"I think you're nice."

Paul turned to her and touched her on the shoulder. "Can I kiss you?"

"I was hoping you would," said Emily.

And they kissed, and it was a giant thing, but it was also quiet, like the biggest moments are. In the room where many poems were once written, Emily sinks to the single bed and cries for all that has been lost, and for all that will be.

· · ·

When Emily lifts her head from the white coverlet, the room is so full of moonlight that she can read by it. She looks at her watch and taps it. There is no way it is only 7:55. She rises from the bed and walks over to the desk chair where the dress is arranged over the back of it as if a person had been sitting there and slipped out for a moment. Did she lay the dress out like that? She was upset, but she doesn't remember doing it. She reaches into the pocket of the dress, feeling for the scrap of paper, which sticks itself, static-like, to her palm. Emily's poetry notebook sits on top of the desk. She doesn't remember putting that there, either. K.T.'s fountain pen rests next to the cover, the moonlight igniting the gold tip. Emily glances at the mannequin, who gazes back.

"Talk to me," Emily says. "You said in one of your poems that you don't believe in heaven. But have you changed your mind? Tell me. Tell me everything."

The mannequin's white lips almost move.

"Is it okay with you if I sit here?" Emily asks. She lowers herself into the chair and peels the scrap of paper from her palm and presses it to the flat surface of the desk, which smells of old wood. She runs both hands along its worn edges and reaches back to touch the dress, thinking of another pocket, the one in a boy's pair of blue jeans, the one that once held a letter from a girl. Whatever happened to that letter? Did Paul burn it? Did he hide it under a mattress or slide it into a chest of treasures or leave it where it landed, a hidden part of a messy pile of laundry?

For minutes, Emily listens to the stillness in the room, which has its own private voice. It tells her that the unexpected maid is not an outside force. She may come as a surprise, yes, but she always comes from within. The maid is the muse, and the girl who discovers her must create for her a world of a meaning in which to live. Under the bright eye of the Cyclops moon, Emily Beam realizes that Emily Dickinson didn't write 1,775 poems just to keep them all to herself. She knew they'd be found. She knew they'd be read. She knew they would prove to other daughters of America, and sons, too, all the survivors, that they are not alone.

Emily Beam opens her notebook to a blank page.

"Pocket," the silence whispers.

"A crib for pencils," Emily whispers back. "A home for matchbooks."

"The night," says the silence. "The whole night is shrinking."

"Once upon a time," says Emily, "this desk was a tree."

"The paper was, too."

"I knew a boy who grew trees. And I think that I loved him."

"Morning fades," says the silence.

"When I die," asks Emily, "where will I go? What dark pocket of time will rock me to sleep?"

POCKET

Crib for pencils   matchbooks
splinters of trees in my apron
restructured trunks all over

the place   My desk once an oak
its rings now blocked
angles of legs and grooves

Paper I write on   past
maple or pine   so many
limbs gone sapless

Time has tucked in
arranged days   waking
sweeping   feeding the cat

washing a plate as moonlight
wanes   reading poems as
the week unfolds

then folds again
Morning fades
I can't recall numbers

count back to zero   stunned
that I came to be born
The whole night is shrinking

trunks and twigs
kindling to ash   the fabric
of sky taken in   Seams

hold only so long then
fray   frazzle   dangle us
all in the dark

When I fall
what pocket
will cradle me?

                    Emily Beam, *March 18, 1995*

EMILY LEAVES THE WHITE DRESS WHERE IT IS AND WHERE, SHE IS SURE, it wants to stay. Feeling as silly as a child, she walks over to the mannequin and says, "I don't believe in heaven, either. But I wish I did." With a last look at the room, Emily carries the earthy weight of herself down the graceful staircase. In the parlor, at the piano, her hands feel their way through the only song they know: "Chopsticks." In the darkness, she can see the outline of the empty boots, which look smaller without her feet in them.

She isn't even sure she'll be able to get out of the house. *Time to pray,* she thinks, and closes her eyes. When she opens them, she walks as quietly as she can to the front door where an old-fashioned key peeks out of the lock. The key turns easily, and out Emily goes, clicking the door shut behind her. She turns the knob to the right, then to the left, but the door is locked. The porch light blinks on and off three times. Emily checks her watch: 9:15.

Across the street on the bench is a silhouette, but it does not belong to Amber. It rises, floating toward her, the pale face of Madame Colche catching the light of the moon. Emily walks slowly down the steps as Madame Colche crosses the street. They meet at the iron gate.

"*Allons,*" says Madame Colche. *Let's go.*

"How did you know I was here?" Emily asks, shivering.

"Call it an educated guess," says Madame Colche.

Emily hunches into herself. "Am I in trouble?"

"*Oui.*"

"Will I be sent home?" She watches her breath make little clouds in the air.

"That remains to be seen," Madame Colche says. "But it's a possibility."

"A possibility or a probability?"

Madame Colche pats Emily on her shoulder. "Shhh. Where's your coat?"

"I left it at school."

"You must be *très froide.*"

"*Je suis,*" Emily says. *I am.*

They walk for two blocks without talking, and then Emily says, "You remember my friend Terra from the train trip who lives in Winesburg, Ohio?"

"*Oui.*"

"I didn't know that was the name of a famous book. Amber told me."

"She is a *font de connaissance,*" says Madame Colche.

"A what?"

"A fountain of knowledge."

"Yeah," says Emily. "She can be. Anyway, have you read it, *Winesburg, Ohio?*"

"I have."

"What's it about?"

"Well, it's a collection of stories about various people living in a small town who are searching for truth, all different kinds," Madame Colche says.

"How many different kinds are there?"

"So many. Too many to count."

Emily looks up at the moon. "Like stars," she says.

"Oui," says Madame Colche. *"Comme les étoiles dans le ciel."*

"That's what her voice sounded like," Emily says.

"Whose voice?"

"Emily Dickinson's. When I was in her house, she spoke to me."

"My dear girl," says Madame Colche, "of course she did."

· · ·

In 15 Hart Hall, Amber and K.T. are waiting, and Emily tells them how she got back.

"I don't know what will happen," she tells them. "Madame Colche and Dr. Ingold and I don't know who all are meeting first thing in the morning."

"Madame Colche came by before dinner to see if we wanted to eat at her house," K.T. says. "That's how she knew you weren't here."

"But I don't know how she knew you were there," Amber says. "We didn't tell her."

"It's okay," says Emily. "It's probably better that she found me. At least that way, I didn't have to lie to anybody."

"And who knows?" says K.T. "She might be able to soften the blow. She's taught here for over twenty years. Dr. Ingold has been here only half that long. People listen to Madame Colche."

"What was it like, being in there at night?" Amber asks. "Was it spooky? I started to ring the doorbell, but I was afraid you'd have a heart attack."

"It was a different kind of spooky," Emily says. "I'll tell you about it sometime, but right now, I have to make a phone call."

"Are they making you call your mom and dad and tell them what you did?" Amber asks. "ASG loves that kind of shit."

"No. I have to call a friend from home."

"I'll walk you out," says Amber. "See you, K.T. Thanks for keeping me company."

K.T. gives Emily a look, but she's smiling. "It was an experience," K.T. says.

For once, the hall phone has no one attached to it. Most of the girls are in the student center watching a marathon of John Hughes films, including *The Breakfast Club,* which was what was playing when Amber came and got K.T. Emily picks up the receiver and dials the number she can't forget and Carey answers on the first ring.

"It's me," Emily says. "Are you alone?"

"Mom and Dad are asleep in the den," says Carey.

"I'm alone, too," Emily says. "Finally. Sorry I haven't called before now."

"It's okay."

"It's not okay," says Emily, "but thank you for saying so. I have a feeling that I know why you called."

"You do?"

Emily takes a deep breath. "You found the letter."

"Yeah," Carey says. "In the pocket of Paul's pants."

"Did you tell your parents?"

"What's the point? It would just have made everyone sadder than they already are," Carey says.

"That was nice of you," says Emily.

"I didn't do it for them."

"How did you know the letter was there?"

"I didn't," Carey says. "I went into Paul's room the night after he died, looking for something, anything, I don't know. His clothes were lying there on the floor, waiting for him to take them to the laundry room. It was so final. He wouldn't be back to do that, so I did it for him, and that's how I found it."

Emily knows what she must say. It's not the nicest way to handle it, but Emily has had enough of nice. Look where nice has gotten her.

"I wouldn't have gotten back together with Paul," Emily says. "I know it says so in the letter, but I don't think I could have. I hurt him beyond repair. Burn the letter, Carey. Okay? Burn it."

"I don't know if I can."

"Why not?"

"It was something Paul touched."

"Then send it to me and I'll burn it."

"No," Carey says. "I can do it. He was my big brother."

"Please don't tell anyone, ever, that I was pregnant. Please."

"I won't. Like I said, it would just bring more hurt. We all knew you had broken up with him. It was because of the baby, I know, but do you think that's why he—?"

"I don't know, Carey. But it might be. In which case maybe you *should* tell your parents. At least it might take some of the confusion out of it. And some of the guilt."

"None of us believe that Paul planned to kill himself," says

Carey. "We've talked to the therapist. We've talked to Ms. Albright. It was an impulse. And that's not your fault."

"Yes, it is." Emily starts to cry. "I wouldn't blame you if you hated me. Paul was a really good person. And a really good boyfriend, too. I miss him."

"I miss him, too."

"Maybe we can get together and talk when I come home for spring break?"

"I don't hate you," Carey says. "And, yes, let's. And, Emily, your secret is safe. I promise. Paul would have wanted it that way."

Emily knows she will always remember Paul, but she isn't sure where it is he will stay. She hopes he'll stay in her head. She will need room in her heart for other things, other people. She tells Carey goodbye for now and walks back down the hall to the room, where K.T. is about to jump out of her skin. She hands Emily a piece of notebook paper.

Dear Poet,
*   Your poem "Mother, Once Removed" has been entered*
into the Emily Dickinson Poetry Contest.
*   Love,*
*   Your Friends on Hart Hall*

Emily rushes over to the bed and runs her hand under the mattress. She looks under the bed. The poem is gone. She dumps the contents of the trash can on the floor. The balled-up entry form is gone, too, the one she marked all over.

"Annabelle and Waverley," Emily tells K.T. "Payback

time. Amber saw Annabelle coming out of our room today. She stole my poem."

"Which one?"

"My secret one. God, I am so screwed. They're going to broadcast it to the entire school."

"Maybe not," K.T. says. "What's the poem about?"

"My abortion." On a sheet of paper, she jots down some of the lines she remembers and shows them to K.T.

"I don't think you need to worry," K.T. says. "If they think they've got something on you, you can just be mysterious and say it's all metaphor."

Emily laughs a little laugh.

"Who knows? Maybe they were trying to be nice," K.T. says. "Turn over a new leaf. It can happen."

"Annabelle was snooping around in my room," says Emily. "I don't think she was doing that to be nice."

"Well, if you win, the pizza's on you for the rest of the year."

"I won't win," says Emily. "I'm not the winning type."

K.T. offers a sad smile. "You can probably get the poem pulled out of the contest if you want to, right? But maybe you don't want to."

"I think I've written better ones," Emily says. "Clearer ones. Tell me the truth. Do you think I'm a bad person for what I did?"

"Well, Emily Beam Me Up Scotty, here's what I think. If God made us in His image, then maybe we have a right to play God when we can't find Him anywhere. But we will find Him, eventually. It's what my pastor told us after Caroline died."

"He sounds smart."

"She," K.T. says. "Yeah, Reverend Fairfax is brilliant. She went to Harvard. Where you will go, too. Especially if you win the contest. You never know—Annabelle and Waverley might have done you a huge favor."

"They were doing it to be mean," Emily says.

"I wouldn't be so sure."

"Well, Doubt *is* my middle name."

"What *is* your middle name?"

"Elizabeth."

"Oooo. Can I start calling you 'e. e.'?"

Emily laughs. "Please don't."

"e. e. beam." K.T. claps her hands. "How about 'eeb'?"

"How about just Emily?"

"Just Emily. Kind of like Madonna, but humbler. Yeah, that's perfect for you."

"You might have to call me Exit Emily after tomorrow."

K.T. walks over to Emily's bed and sits down beside her. "They'll want to keep you," she says. "You're an ASG girl through and through. They're going to want you to stay."

CLOUDS

Girl curled up
    in a brown field
        watching the sky:

I will die
    too, she thinks
        with all of my

memories
    huddled like quilts
        on a messy bed

I'll be remade
    a cloud changing
        shape

unicorn
    cornucopia
        piano

My mother and father
    will ask God
        where I am

but He cannot
    find a lone child
        in the vast

white parade
    Too many clouds
        shifting fast

in the millions
of miles of
blue everlasting

Emily Beam, *March 19, 1995*

ON SUNDAY MORNING, EMILY WAKES TO A COLD, HARD RAIN. K.T. IS still asleep. Emily checks the clock. They still have time to get to the dining room before breakfast ends, before she is summoned to Dr. Ingold's office to accept her punishment.

She gets out of bed and shakes K.T.'s shoulder. "I'm hungry," she says. "And I'm scared. Let's go eat."

K.T. rolls over. "Two minutes," she says. She flips on the radio, and the girls get dressed to classical music. Back in Grenfell County, Emily didn't care for Mozart and Beethoven and all those powder-wigged composers, but she is learning to respect the complexity of their work. K.T. is teaching her about music, just as she is teaching K.T. about Emily Dickinson.

"All right, Poet Girl," says K.T. "I'm ready, so grab that umbrella, and leave those other boots behind. You're going to need your rain boots." Emily does as K.T. says, but as they push through the heavy door of their dorm and onto the quad, the rain turns to snow.

"No way!" yells Emily.

"It's snowing!" shouts K.T. "One day before spring!" She grabs Emily's hand, and they jump up and down like children out of school, which brings to mind mittens and sleds,

Boston and history, Tchaikovsky's "Waltz of the Flowers" and Dickinson's alabaster chambers. By the time Emily and K.T. have finished breakfast, the snow has covered the pebbly sidewalks and the tallest stubs of grass. On the way back to 15 Hart Hall, they pass girls making snow angels, and without a word to one another, K.T. and Emily lie on their backs side by side, sliding their arms and legs back and forth.

The hard part, as any girl knows, is standing back up without ruining your angel. K.T. makes a mess of hers and laughs. "Oh, look, Em," she says, pointing. "Yours is perfect." Emily turns around to admire the mark she has made on the whiteness. She smiles at the metaphor. *I* am *a poet,* she thinks to herself. *Oh, my God, I really am.* She lifts her face to the sky, the snow soft as kisses. She and K.T. walk back to Hart Hall with upturned faces, holding on to one another's hands for balance.

When they pass 12 Hart Hall, Emily knocks on the door and pokes her head in. Annabelle and Waverley are sitting on their beds.

"Hey, girls!" Emily waves. "Thank you! That was super, super nice of you. I hope I win!" She closes the door, and she and K.T. fall into a fit of giggles. When they open their own door, they squeal with delight. A large canvas rests on Emily's desk. The painting of a yellow house with white columns manages to be both realistic and impressionistic.

"Amber painted it," Emily says.

"How in the heck did she do that so fast? It's amazing."

"Amber, my crazy friend."

"So what does that make me?" K.T. asks, raising her eyebrows. "I'm your crazy friend, too, right?"

"No," Emily says.

"Knock, knock," says Madame Colche, standing at the open door. "Dr. Ingold is ready for you, Emily. You'd better bring some work with you in case you have to wait."

Emily slings her book bag over her shoulder. Before she follows her French teacher down the stairs, Emily kisses K.T. on the cheek and says, "You're not my crazy friend. You're my best friend."

. . .

But best friends can be separated by miles and miles, Emily thinks as she walks with Madame Colche to Dr. Ingold's office.

> Wintertime keeps hanging
> To every twig and blade
> Hiding all the green
> So girls can't find their way.

In silence, she is ushered in to sit in the high-backed chair. Her spine straight as a pencil, Emily focuses her gaze past Dr. Ingold's head, waiting for the cuckoo to pop out and tell her what she already knows, that in one minute, it will be ten o'clock. At least she knows something. Madame Colche sits in a chair by the window, her elegant hands folded neatly in her lap. With a stern voice, Dr. Ingold doles out Emily's jail sentence, which will be delivered to her parents in a phone call from the headmistress. No, Emily Elizabeth Beam will not be expelled, but she is campused for the rest of the year.

No dances with boys' schools, no strolls down Main Street, no cemeteries, no drugstores, no smoking, no Emily Dickinson House. She is assigned to ten hours a week of unpaid work with the grounds crew, keeping the lawns and campus flower beds looking fresh all spring long.

After Dr. Ingold finishes, Emily puts her head in her hands and sobs. Madame Colche almost has to carry her out of the office.

"Why don't you find a quiet place to regroup?" she tells Emily. "I'll let K. T. know."

"I'll be in the lieberry," Emily says, gulping for air.

"Lieberry?"

"*Oui*. Remind me to explain it to you sometime."

Emily's knees shake all the way to her carrel. She is so relieved that she sits and cries out every tear inside of her. When she can see clearly, Emily reads back through the poems, changing a word here, a line break there. She will type up the poems and send copies in an envelope to Ms. Albright. It's time. She walks over to a long table and spreads the poems out. It is a lot to take in, a lot to get over, and a lot to share with Ms. Albright, but for now, for the present, Emily keeps her words to herself. They are good, they are true, and they bear no one else's touch but her own. No help from a psychiatrist or a teacher, no parent looking over her shoulder, offering suggestions. Emily Beam has gone it alone.

Or maybe halfway alone. She owes some of it to Paul. Emily moves thirty poems around like tiles—a white path she will walk across to a green world—and gives them their final order. She puts them in pairs so they can talk to one another: her little book is a love story, after all, and lovers argue and question; they give and take, sidestep and hide, retreat and advance. On paper, they reunite for the duration.

First "Blues." Then "Buttons."

"Seed" goes with "Sew," (now that it's found).

"Girl at a Bedroom Window" and "The Meeting."

"The Traveling Show" with "Conception."

"Pall" and "Mosaics."

"Shroud" with "The Doctor."

"Maze" and "Never Land."

"The Safe Way" with "Little Sister."

"Small Things" and "Pocket."

"The Shell" and "Hold Up."

"Poem of the Middle Heart" with "Me and You and God."

"A New Solar System" with "Robin's Egg."

"Absinthe" and "Treasures."

"Anthology" and "DNA."

"Clouds" at the beginning, all by itself, and "Ashes" here at the end.

And the poem under her mattress, "Mother, Once Removed," will stay removed. It may sit for weeks in a pile of mail, and whether it ends up on the bottom of a recycling bin or on the top of a heap, it is its own entity. Its own pocket in time. It does not have to define who Emily is, was, or will be.

Yes, Emily thinks, *this is the right order; this is how they will go.*

She binds the poems together with a blue ribbon and a title, *Clouds.*

This is how they will go.
This is how she will go: on.
The light almost speaking,
and March halfway gone,
the green fields beyond,
and the staying.

ACKNOWLEDGMENTS

At the 2012 meeting of the Emily Dickinson International Society, a possible new daguerreotype was brought to light. If confirmed as authentic, it will stand as only the second image of Dickinson known to exist. If you would like to see it or the more well-known image that haunts Emily Beam, visit emilydickinsonmuseum.org.

From this excellent website, I gathered details for my story and checked facts. I also used *Lives Like Loaded Guns: Emily Dickinson and Her Family's Feuds* by Lyndall Gordon; *My Wars Are Laid Away in Books: The Life of Emily Dickinson* by Alfred Habegger; *The Gardens of Emily Dickinson* by Judith Farr (with Louise Carter); and a delightful children's book titled, simply, *Emily* by Michael Bedard, with illustrations by Barbara Cooney.

The Complete Poems of Emily Dickinson (edited by Thomas H. Johnson) sat on my desk as I wrote. So thank you, Emily Dickinson, for your unforgettable voice and all of the words you have lent me.

I also extend my gratitude to

Jonathan Lyons, my hero-agent;

Michelle Poploff and Rebecca Short, my editors in shining armor;

Sally Hubbard Hawn, my go-to reader, always;

Polly Adkins, Stephanie O'Neill, Denise Stewart, and Ford Thomson, for their various inputs, as well as Alexandra King and the rest of the girls in Proal Heartwell's 2011–2012 eighth-grade English class at Village School in Charlottesville, Virginia;

Jayne and Joel Hubbard, my parents;

and Steve Cobb, husband of gold, who makes my writing life possible.

ABOUT THE AUTHOR

And We Stay is Jenny Hubbard's second novel. Her first, *Paper Covers Rock,* was a finalist for the William C. Morris YA Debut Award. A former English teacher, Jenny writes books and plays in her hometown of Salisbury, North Carolina, where she lives with her husband, a high school math teacher, and their rescue dog, Oliver. You can find Jenny on Facebook, follow her (and Oliver) on Twitter at @HubbardWrites, and visit her website at jennyhubbard.com.